THE DSA SEASON TWO, BOOK SIX

TERMINAL POINT

Also by Lou Paduano

The Greystone Saga

Signs of Portents

Tales from Portents

The Medusa Coin

Pathways in the Dark

A Circle of Shadows

Greystone-in-Training

Hammer and Anvil

The Gifts of Kali

The Final Gauntlet

The DSA

Season One

The Clearing

Promethean

The Bridge

Spectral Advocate

Dark Impulses

Broken Loyalties

Season Two

The Wellspring

Foundations

The Missing

Cracked Chrysalis

Secret Histories

THE DSA SEASON TWO, BOOK SIX

TERMINAL POINT

Lou Paduano

Eleven Ten Publishing LLC

GRAND ISLAND, NEW YORK

Eleven Ten Publishing LLC
282 Fareway Lane
Grand Island, NY 14072

Publisher's note: This is a work of fiction. Names, characters, places, and incidents either are the product of the author's imagination or are used fictitiously. Any resemblance to actual events, locales, or persons, living or dead, is entirely coincidental.

Printed in the United States of America
Edited by JP Services.
Cover art design by MiblArt

First edition published 2024

Library of Congress Cataloguing in Publication Data
Paduano, Lou
Terminal Point / Lou Paduano

LCCN: 2024920118
ISBN-13: 978-1-944965-47-1 (paperback)
ISBN-13: 978-1-944965-46-4 (eBook)

For Vicki

CHAPTER ONE

"This is it."

The car cruised to a halt along the corner of Woodbine and Plymouth. Passenger-side tires hugged the curb. The hum of the engine ran in the background against the sound of birds fluttering overhead. The late-morning sun washed over the skyline, but downtown spires blotted out the impressive light, casting deep shadows on the streets below.

The shadows covered Zac Modine's face. The wide-brimmed cap he'd borrowed from the man behind the wheel helped to obscure him from the traffic cams that lined every block of Bismarck.

"You sure this is the place?" Buck asked. He was well into his fifties, with bushy eyebrows that hid his muted green eyes.

Zac had met the man at a diner in the wee hours of the morning. His travels from the Trust compound had been frantic and scattered. For every mile in the right direction, Zac had taken three to cover his tracks from any potential pursuer. From bus routes to taxi cabs, over the course of the last two days, he had done everything possible to make it to Bismarck safely. Since learning about the destination, the city had called to him—another voice added to the mix in his mind.

Buck had immediately noticed Zac in the diner. With no money, and a pair of clothes begging to be changed, Zac had been easy to spot and easier to ignore. Zac's appearance hadn't bothered Buck. He brought the weary traveler a plate of food he'd ordered for the road and joined him for a meal and a story. Zac had declined to share most of his tale, but when he mentioned Bismarck as his ultimate destination, Buck had been gracious enough to take him the rest of the way.

A change of clothes later—the man's generosity knew no bounds—and they had started their trek. Buck had filled the trip, and the silence from his companion, with his own stories. They had been tales of loss and great sacrifice, but through each one, Buck carried a joy in his voice that never diminished.

Zac was grateful to the man—both for his deeds and his words. They lightened the load burdening his mind. They eased the journey that troubled him for so long. Peace returned to his thoughts and his dreams... until they arrived at their destination.

"Zac? I said, you sure this is the place?"

"This is it, yes," Zac said.

Buck turned to the window, his furrowed brow stuck in place. "Looks abandoned. In fact, I've been coming down this way for years, and it's always looked that way to me. Like whoever owned it just forgot about it one day. And then so did everyone else."

"Buck?" Zac stared at him curiously. "Are you sure we're looking at the same place?"

"On the corner, right?" Buck asked. "Place is practically falling apart. Why the city hasn't done anything to clean it up, considering everything else in the area, makes no sense to me."

Zac didn't understand what Buck meant. Where Buck saw a rotting derelict, Zac beheld a wonder. The building sparkled in the sunlight. The spire shot up into the sky like a rocket. Their perceptions failed to line up. Unfortunately for Zac, that was becoming the norm, and he kept the truth to himself.

He patted Buck on the shoulder. "I can't thank you enough for everything."

"I'm happy to do more," Buck said. "You don't have to stand alone. Whatever it is you've got going on, there are people willing to help. I—"

"I know." Zac stopped the man with a sad smile. His silence afforded him nothing but more concern from the man. This trip, however, was for Zac to complete. "Trust me, Buck. I know I'm not alone in this."

"Call me," Buck said. "You need anything, you call."

"Thank you." Zac took the man's hand, gave a firm shake, and then stepped out of the car. Zac offered a goodbye wave.

Buck, for a second, appeared ready to join his departed passenger. He held tight to the door handle. His eyes locked on the building across the street. The second they did, his fingers started to tremble until he let go of the door and settled against his seat. Then the Good Samaritan shifted the car to drive and coasted into the morning traffic. A gentle nod of farewell left Zac to the task ahead.

Zac crossed the street at the light. He slipped between pedestrians, who rushed to their destinations. The crowd headed to places of employment, or off to an early lunch, while shoppers moved slightly slower to head to their next excursion.

None stopped at the building on the corner of the busy intersection. Not a single one even looked toward it in passing. Something about the place sent them heading in the opposite direction, as if commanded to ignore the gleaming structure.

Only Zac appeared to witness the truth: he finally arrived at his journey's end. He had spent too long getting here, too many agonizing weeks on a trek that had seen him chased, beaten, and abused by too many outside parties. All had been interested in the Wellspring, and the secret behind its protocol: the signal.

Inside were the answers to that mysterious item. According to the voice locked in his mind, the signal stood at the center of everything—every innovation and advancement of the last century and beyond. The signal gave birth to the future, one Zac needed to stop from happening.

It was the only way to save his life, and the only way he could ever reunite with his family again. Nothing would stop him from fulfilling that goal. Zac's fists balled up at his sides, and he started for the front door.

"No turning back now."

CHAPTER TWO
Three Hours Earlier

Claire barely felt her legs under her. Her hands were numb, and her bladder was full. Her extended stay in the air ducts of the Trust compound left her dehydrated and terrified. Every noise she'd heard during her stay had caused her to cringe in terror. Every shift of her weight along the tight quarters of her hiding place had boomed in her ears, and she'd waited to be found out by the men hunting her.

None had come. No one had bothered to even search for her as far as she could tell from her vantage point. There had only been the darkness to keep her company.

Sleep had been a waste of time. Every time she'd tried to drift off, a sudden spasm would rock her awake. Anxiety had taken over after that, more than enough to keep her on edge during her thirty-six-hour visit. When seven in the morning came, Claire prepared to depart.

Her window was limited. A gap in the security, according to her husband, occurred at 7:43 on Wednesday. His instructions had been limited, but extremely specific as to her escape route. She took the vent back to the elevator shaft. Traveling to the ground floor, she found an access tube toward the southern exit. The construction made it easier to slip back into the main building, where she waited for her allotted time.

At the appointed minute, two guards split from the exit to begin their patrol of the perimeter. Claire shook her head in disbelief, shocked at the precision of her husband's prediction. The door opened under her care, and Claire stepped into the light.

She was careful not to run—another edict from her husband.

Zac's voice pushed her forward and soothed the blinding terror that came with each movement. Every turn frightened her, every choice laced with imagined foes and the chilling sound of screams and gunfire. Her life was on the line. So was Zac's.

Four blocks disappeared behind her. The sun stayed at her back, and she refused to veer from the path set before her. Claire kept her eyes low and steady on the sidewalk. She offered no glances back to the compound, or to the neighboring crossroads. She focused all her energy on fulfilling her husband's wishes.

The diner sat right where Zac had said—four blocks west of the Trust building. The OPEN sign hung in the doorway, and a small crowd gathered within. It was the only business on the block welcoming people at such an early hour.

How did Zac know?

The question plagued her every step of the way. Zac had never been to the area, not for as long as she had known him at least. Had he lied about that? If so, what else was he lying about?

No, she thought with the shake of her head. Doubting Zac had brought them to this moment. He had certainly made his share of mistakes in the past, and they stung worse than any dagger in the back could. She might not have forgiven him for his betrayal, however, her love for Zac remained just as real as ever. That faith carried her forward.

Claire stepped up to the door and pulled it from the frame to enter. She stood in the doorway for a long moment to scan the patrons for signs of recognition. Her fear took over, and with each individual, she no longer saw the smiles on their faces or heard their laughter over coffee and breakfast. To her, everyone was a danger and a delay from her task.

Pushing past her terror, Claire found the payphone waiting in the back corner of the diner. An elderly woman sat in front of the device, her feet resting on a borrowed stool for comfort. She paid no mind to the approaching woman, or to anyone else, as evidenced by the cigarette dangling from her lips despite the signage throughout the place.

"Ma'am?" Claire stopped short of the woman's position. "I need to use the phone."

The woman continued to talk through the line. She clearly held no interest in listening to whoever might be on the other side of the call.

Claire's bladder threatened to burst. The tension throughout her body caused her fingers to curl and her nails to dig into her thighs. She inched closer. "Ma'am?"

"One minute," the woman barked.

Claire closed her eyes. She forced a breath, then two. The woman, however, continued to gab incessantly, while ash piled on the surrounding floor.

"I don't have a minute," Claire said, her voice louder this time. She reached for the woman's shoulder.

The woman pulled back, clutching tight to the receiver. "Wait your turn."

Claire seethed. She fought through the exhaustion and terror that plagued her entire body. Patience at an end, Claire plucked the cigarette from the woman's lips. She jammed the foul-smelling stick into the side of the phone to blot it out, then let it fall among the ashes.

"Hang up," Claire said. "Now."

The woman grumbled, then rolled her eyes. She sat up. "Whatever. Yeah… I'll call you back." She slammed the receiver down. Standing, the woman backed away, hands in the air with frustration. "It's all yours, your majesty."

"Thank you," Claire said in her best teacher voice.

The woman flipped her off. "Bite me."

Claire lifted the receiver to hear the dial tone in her ear. Relief washed over her as she settled against the wall. She pulled a slip of paper from her pocket. Zac's handwriting brought a smirk to her lips. Taking the number from the hurried instructions, Claire entered the digits on the keypad. She messed up twice, her fingers shaky from the long night, but eventually she entered the correct number.

It rang twice before someone picked up. "This is Morgan."

Claire's eyes widened. Her heart nearly leaped from her chest.

"Hello?"

"M… Morgan?" Claire said. "Morgan Dunleavy?"

Claire couldn't find her voice. On the other end of the line was the woman Zac had slept with. Morgan had been the reason for their separation, for the pain of the last two months. She had destroyed their lives, yet she was the one Zac turned to for help?

Tears stung her cheeks. Claire slid to the floor, the receiver still tight to her ear.

"Yes," the woman replied. "This is Morgan. Who is this? How did you get this number?"

From your lover. Not Claire's husband. Zac had never desired Claire like he had Morgan. Claire covered the speaker. "Of course it would be her."

Part of her wanted nothing more than to hang up and let the chips fall where they may. That feeling came from anger at being betrayed by her husband, while stupidly still loving him. The same part of her wanted to kick and scream at the woman on the line for all the trouble she had brought into Claire's life.

Zac, however, needed her to be stronger than that. She needed to be better than some scorned woman. Truthfully, while he might have turned to Morgan for backup, Zac also required help from Claire to make it happen. To be a family again, to put the past behind them and make a go at forgiveness, Claire needed to work with Morgan.

"Hello?" Morgan called into the line once more.

"It's Claire, Morgan." She swiped away her tears. "Claire Modine."

"Claire?" Morgan asked, concern in her voice. "What is it? Is Zac—"

"He's in trouble," Claire said. "Zac needs your help."

CHAPTER THREE

It had been a rough night. Ben rubbed at weary eyes as he entered the Operations Hub of the Bunker. Against his better judgment, coffee was in the offering. He needed a pot of the disgusting concoction to push through the blinding headache that came from his sleepless night. At the sight of Morgan at the conference table, all forward momentum ground to a halt.

She had been the reason for his lack of sleep. Not directly, though. That would have been something completely different and a welcome diversion. No, his insomnia was merely a case of an active mind. Ever since their time in the freezer—trapped by a sociopath out for revenge—whenever Ben contemplated the subject of his partner, there was something new thrown in the mix.

They had worked together for months, but for the first time, Ben saw her in a new light. Out of all the reasons he might stay with the DSA, Morgan topped the list. He wanted to be there for her... and *with* her. The revelation staggered him. He had spent his every effort searching for Emily Wright, his former partner—an unrequited love from his time in Buffalo. Yet, was there a reason the pair never said anything to each other? Was there a reason they stopped at a certain point, maintaining a friendship over something deeper? He still loved Emily, missed her and desired her safe return to the world but, more than that? Ben was no longer sure. His time with the DSA had changed him, opened new possibilities to him.

Realizing Morgan had been the driving force for his continued stay with the DSA made it clear there was more to their time together than Ben had imagined possible. She meant something to him beyond the work at hand, his dreams clearly understanding his own troubled mind better than he ever could. The thought of being with Morgan, of deepening their relationship beyond the joking and danger that consumed their day-to-day lives, had hit him so hard sleep became impossible. So was talking to Morgan about it, as he skirted along the edge of the room rather than pass her position on the floor.

It was juvenile avoidance behavior—his specialty in life. Ben cursed himself for not being honest about this new perception of their time together. He feared the reprisal of such a change. And there was still Emily to consider...

Pouring a steaming cup of coffee from the pot, Ben sat along the kitchen counter. He sipped at the dark sludge. Each swallow brought a wince to his face. Sure, coffee was a necessary evil in life, but why couldn't it at least taste decent without a mountain of sugar and cream thrown into the mix?

Morgan continued to sit at the conference room table. She ran a hand through her lush curls. With a phone to her ear, Morgan leaned over the table to listen intently to the voice on the other end of the line. Her words were muffled, but Ben caught the end of the conversation.

"We'll find him," Morgan said. "You have my word."

She hung up the phone, cradling the device in her hand. Morgan stared off at the blank monitors surrounding her, clearly lost to a memory drawn by the call.

Ben's trepidation gave way to mounting concern. He stood, walked over to the metal stairs, and stopped at the landing. "Morgan?" he called. "Who was that?"

Tucking the phone away, Morgan drew her hair back and tied it off. She started up the steps toward him. "Zac is in trouble," she said. "Hollis is after him, and Claire... Zac's wife called us for help."

Zac's wife. The way she said it made the look on her face all the more clear. The past slammed into them both like a bullet to the brain. Morgan was lost to the memory of her tryst with Zac. That was Ben's word for it, though he understood the brief affair had been something far more to his partner.

Morgan wanted more with Zac. She wanted to have more from him than just a fling. Life, however, interfered and split them apart as quickly as it had brought them together.

Ben had nearly forgotten about their relationship. The shock on Morgan's face over her call with Claire Modine was nothing compared to the brutal slap to Ben's cheek. It woke him up to the reality of his situation. Morgan obviously still felt something for Zac.

He stopped her at the landing, a gentle hand on her arm. "Hey. I know Zac is a touchy subject around here, but if he's in danger, nothing is going to stop us from helping."

Morgan nodded. She cleared her throat and stood taller to shake off the remaining effects of her call.

"So, what's going on?" Ben asked.

Morgan led him to the kitchen and the still steaming pot of coffee. "She didn't know much. Claire sounded in shock. The only thing I understood was a location."

"It's a start," Ben said, following behind. "Where are we going, and please say Oahu?"

"You wish," Morgan replied with a smirk. She poured a cup of coffee, then let it warm the palms of her hands. "No, it's Bi—"

"BISMARCK!"

Both turned in confusion at the new voice in the room. Alison Adler rushed toward them. Her arms were raised high in the air, like she was taking a victory lap around the underground complex.

"—smarck," Morgan finished. "Wait. What?"

Adler stopped before them, her brow furrowed. "How did you know?"

"Why did you say Bismarck?" Morgan asked.

"Why did *you* say Bismarck?"

Ben lowered his coffee to the counter and covered his ears. "Please make this stop."

Morgan slapped his arm. "Baby." She turned away from him and took a long sip of her drink before asking, "What did you find, Adler?"

Adler could barely stand still. Her feet shuffled along the floor. Her hands shook before her. "Okay, remember that signal that cropped up when the Cove imploded? I ran search after search to trace some kind of destination, or source, from the thing."

Morgan knew the story better than Ben, considering she had been at the Cove when the hill collapsed over the futuristic structure. Both, however, had heard plenty about Adler's mysterious signal since her initial discovery.

"Which is why you were resetting the system when Vivian Ness decided to drop by for a visit, and some revenge on Metcalf." Morgan pushed the excited analyst through her tale.

"Right." Adler smiled. Small hops were joined by clapping hands at her joy. "It worked."

"You found the source of the signal?" Surprise filled Ben's voice. The reset gave their impressive mainframe enough power to catch up to the elusive signal, but after hours there had appeared to be no progress in the search.

"Not the source," Adler clarified. "A relay point. But it's a start."

She pulled her tablet out from under her arm. Tapping the screen brought the device back to life. A map was on full display. Bismarck, North Dakota, was locked in the center.

"That's where Claire said we were going?" Ben asked Morgan.

She offered a slight nod and took the tablet in hand. "The signal happens to be right where Zac is at this very moment?"

"I have a bad feeling about this," Ben said in a deep voice. At the impression, Morgan shook her head. Adler crossed her arms, all excitement wiped away. Ben looked at both of them. "What? No love for Harrison Ford?"

Morgan scoffed. "Too much to let you disgrace him like that."

Adler agreed with a huff.

"Whatever," Ben grumbled. "When do we leave for Bismarck?"

"Maybe after we answer our front door?" Nixon Jessup said upon entering the room. He hugged a laptop to his chest, his eyes bleary from what appeared to be another long night without sleep. What the man worked on might have been a mystery, but his constant diligence had certainly been an asset to the team.

Everyone turned to him, unsure of his meaning. Nixon sighed, then took to the stairs and the monitors below. A quick tapping along the keys brought the screens to life, the subject displayed on each one with a current timestamp in the corner.

A lone figure stood outside the Bunker's main door. Twin

suitcases rested next to his feet. Pushing up a thin set of glasses, the man known as Simon Holbrook leaned closer to the camera, which gave the team a full view of the man's nostrils.

Nixon smirked. "It appears we have company."

CHAPTER FOUR

David Hollis disliked the distraction. When the call had arrived—more like a demand—Hollis had been in the middle of project updates from a dozen different facilities positioned around the globe. The Utopia Protocol took top priority, of course, but beyond that were infrastructure deals in no less than three third-world countries, and the transportation agreement with the European Union, which would bring in much needed capital to fund future endeavors. The updates were part of a daily routine and spoke to the broad scope of the Trust's operations.

His operations.

No matter how many members claimed leadership, no matter the voices on the so-called Inner Council of the Trust, all decisions passed through Hollis alone. He had taken the mantle from Anson Greene—his predecessor and mentor for more years than Hollis cared to admit. Their dream had been simplistic: to save humanity from ruin, while controlling the outcome.

That dream grew more complicated as time passed. Questions cropped up with frequent alarm. Most, though, came from the others in the group. Hollis had become little more than their answer-man, their need for more of his precious time like a child wanting attention from a busy parent.

He despised the call, but accepted it nonetheless. At their instruction, Hollis entered his office at Compound 243 and closed the door behind him. Sitting in his chair, Hollis pulled up to his desk. A small switch on the side activated under his delicate touch. The room dropped to complete darkness. A helmet lowered from the ceiling, and Hollis pulled it over his head. Scanners whirred to life. They captured his image and transferred it through the heads-up display.

A virtual-reality conference room opened up before his senses. So real to life, Hollis could feel the chill in the surrounding air as much as he could smell the sweat from the others gathered. Twelve appeared in the room. All held power and control in their hands the way most people clutched the remote for their television. Together, the men and women in the room contained more wealth than most of the planet combined.

Hollis hated them all, yet their usefulness to the mission kept a false smile plastered to his face. "Ladies and gentlemen," he declared. The images of the others flickered in the virtual environment, yet all stared toward him in wait. "My apologies for any delays in attending. How may I address your concerns today?"

"Cut the crap, David," a man in the back said. At the sound of his voice, his relative position shifted closer to Hollis. Malcolm Richards always spoke first. He believed that need came from a position of prestige within the group. Hollis knew it better as nothing more than the act of a grandstanding showman with no true talent for the task. "You know why we've called this meeting."

"Do I?" Hollis said coyly.

"You are making too much noise," Richards continued. "The incident in Grand Island? The loss of the Cove and our man at the NSA? Our work is exposed."

"Not of my making," Hollis replied. "You placed Gregory Sullivan at the DSA, Mr. Richards. Against my recommendations, by the way. You provided him access to information meant for only a few. The few in this room."

Hollis let the silence speak for him. The pause allowed each member to turn toward Richards. The accusation had been true: Richards, through some decades-old fealty to Sullivan, had paved the way for the man's appointment to the Deputy Director position at the DSA. Stallworth had backed the play and had fallen in the end because of the ill-considered choice.

Satisfied at the glowers offered by the rest of the room, Hollis continued. "Cleaning up that mess has taken time. Now, finally, we stand at the edge of something far greater."

"Another dreamer," Richards said with a huff. "Like Anson."

The mention of his mentor and dearly departed friend caused

Hollis to scowl. "Anson Greene brought you to this table. All of you. He found the opportunities that have allowed you and your families to prosper beyond your wildest dreams."

Marybeth Black, a pharmaceutical magnate, pushed her avatar forward with the clearing of her throat. Hollis tried to look away. The woman had seen better days, using more and more of her products over the years. Age frightened away her youth. It drove her every decision.

"Make no mistake, David, we are content with our work."

"You mean your money," Hollis shot back. He didn't need the false compliments. They were as much a waste of time as the meeting. "Work is a foreign concept for each of you. Others labor. You spend."

"Still your tongue, boy," Richards snapped. "The Trust—"

"Is mine." Hollis stood, and his avatar grew in relative size with his anger. "I brought the Wellspring to you, allowing you unfettered access to her information. Giving you advancements in technology beyond your imagination. This room is proof of that."

Marybeth shrank from his rage, a finger raised to make her point. "We have heard reports of the woman's death."

"Yes, David," Richards said. "The Wellspring is dead."

"Yet lives again," Hollis answered with a satisfied smile. Hollis opened his hand. From out of the center of his palm, a display grew. It showed the image of a lone man: the key to their future. "This is Zachary Modine. The new Wellspring."

"How?" Richards said in dismay. "How is this possible?"

Hollis closed his hand. "This is not the end. We've always known the risks of our work. Of whom we were placing our trust in by promoting the Wellspring's advancements as our own. We imagined ourselves humanity's benefactors, while counting our profits in terms of billions."

"Is there a point, David?"

"We were right to move forward with Utopia, Malcolm," Hollis replied. "A fail-safe against the source of our limitless invention. Now, it might be our last hope."

"What's happened?" Marybeth asked.

"We've been betrayed," Hollis said. "Everything we've been given has been nothing compared to what's been held back."

His hand opened again. This time, his mind accessed the records from his earlier conversation with Zac in that very office two days earlier.

> *"The signal," Zac said. "I can lead you to the signal."*
> *"What signal?"*
> *"One hidden outside the usual bandwidth. One relaying terabytes of information constantly for download and distribution via the Wellspring Protocol."*

Hollis ended the conversation, though he held the image of his hand around Claire Modine's throat for a moment longer. His men had yet to locate her within the building. Her husband still eluded Hollis as well.

Once the image faded, Marybeth shifted forward. "What is this signal? What does it mean?"

"I intend to find out." Murmurs filled the virtual room. Fear and concern took flight. Any deviations caused nothing but panic, when all Hollis saw was opportunity. "Worrying will get you nowhere. We planned for such a situation when the Wellspring presented herself back in '86."

"But Utopia?" Richards' sniveling voice whined.

"Is that not why you are here?" Hollis looked to each of them, but held the longest on Richards. "We've prepared for decades to survive what is to come. Even if the whole of humanity should not."

"You truly believe it will come to that?"

"I believe in my team, and the plans we've created for us all," Hollis said. "We will find out what this signal holds, and the secrets kept by the Wellspring. That is, if we're all agreed on that path?"

Silence settled in the space. Eyes wavered from member to member, afraid to even glance at Hollis.

"I appreciate the support."

Richards reached out into the virtual space. "David, we thought—"

"That you would be dead long before the endgame arrived." Hollis smirked at the man. He straightened his collar and stood. "And you very well might be, Mr. Richards. I'll keep you apprised of the situation."

He removed his helmet before any in the group could protest.

The lights returned to the room. Hollis slammed his hands against the desk. He cared little for their contempt, and less for their unmitigated fear in the face of the unknown.

"Hypocrites," he snarled as he moved for the door. "Cowards, the lot of them."

The moment he stepped out into the hall, a member of his personal guard stepped forward. The man held tight to a global positioning unit.

"Sir?" the guard called. "There's been a development."

All thought to his meeting faded. "He's stopped running?"

The man nodded, then passed along the unit. "Modine's been stationary for well over an hour. He's in Bismarck."

Hollis grinned. "I want two teams armed and ready immediately. Have my jet fueled. We're leaving."

He straightened his tie. The future was within reach. All Hollis had to do was take it.

CHAPTER FIVE

Simon Holbrook stood in the Bunker. Every word in the sentence seemed to fit in Ben's mind, yet when they ran together, they made little to no sense. All he could do was offer a bewildered look to the man, who made sparse attempt to hide his own.

"Simon, meet the DSA," Morgan announced. She stood at Holbrook's side, hopeful and determined to make the new arrival as welcome as possible.

"A pleasure," Holbrook said with a slight wave and a forced smile. His comfort level matched the rest of the crowd.

No one responded. They clearly had been surprised by Holbrook's admission to their secret underground lair—Ben's name for it, but typically only when he held his pinky to his lips like a raving super-villain. No one knew what to make of Holbrook, because not a single one had heard anything about his recruitment.

Ben, however, was aware of the latest addition to the team. Morgan's reasons were sound enough. Holbrook had stuck his neck out for Morgan by running a battery of tests on Ben's blood after receiving a miracle drug that had saved his life. Even though the results proved nothing to be out of the ordinary, Morgan's request had left Holbrook unemployed for not submitting the proper request forms for testing. He had no chance of finding another position because of his troubled past.

It was that part Ben was hung up on. Holbrook's past mistakes were a mystery, and after all the secrets held by Metcalf, Ben worried what new drama might develop from inviting a total stranger to the club.

Morgan's gaze thinned at them. "Don't everyone welcome him at once or anything."

Kanigher's arms crossed his chest, and a frustrated sigh slipped from his lips. Adler and Nixon watched on from the kitchen area. They sipped at their coffee with delight, like twin spectators at a sporting event.

Ben rolled his eyes as he approached. He stuck out his hand. "Good to see you again, Holbrook."

Holbrook shook the hand, his earnest smile grateful at the gesture. "And you with your shirt on."

Adler and Nixon's stares widened. Both lowered their cups to the counter and leaned closer to listen. Ben dropped the man's hand. "Let the gossip begin," he muttered.

Morgan grumbled. His juvenile antics always pushed her buttons. Ben tried to tone them down, his mouth unable to agree. Getting closer, building a meaningful dialogue with Morgan, was important to move forward, yet Ben continued to stand in his own way.

Morgan pointed around the room. "That's Alison Adler, operations specialist. Nixon Jessup, tech guru, and Robert—"

Kanigher stopped her with a raised hand. "Is this a smart move, Morgan?"

"Kanigher, I—"

"Who the hell is this guy?" Kanigher continued. "Where do you get off bringing in a total stranger to our operation?"

"Says the guy formerly working for the enemy," Ben commented. Ben closed his eyes the second the words escaped. It wasn't his place to step between Morgan and Kanigher during their little tiff, and his wit certainly didn't win any favors from either party.

"For Susan," Kanigher snapped. "My work for the NSA was for her. She hasn't been gone two days, and you've managed to fill her spot."

"That's not what this is," Morgan said.

Holbrook backed toward the entrance. "I should probably—"

Morgan grabbed him by the sleeve. "No, Simon. You stay."

"Yeah," Ben said. He stepped up to Kanigher. The man stood four inches taller than Ben, his frame wider through years of training. Ben refused to back down. "If Kanigher has a problem, I can always beat it out of him."

Kanigher leaned close, fury in his eyes. "I would love to see you try, Riley. The only muscle you seem to exercise is that mouth of yours."

"Thirty minutes of stretches every morning before breakfast," Ben replied. Adler and Nixon immediately started laughing. Ben shook his head. "Great. More gossip."

"Can't you take anything seriously?" Kanigher said with a groan. "Don't answer that. I have an op to prep."

Kanigher started for Operations. Ben felt his fists tighten at his sides. He stamped his foot. "No."

Kanigher halted at the top of the steps. He turned his head back. "No?"

"That's right," Ben said. "No."

"I have more combat experience that anyone here."

"And Morgan has more DSA experience," Ben shot back. From the periphery, Ben noticed the woman's eyes spark at the mention of her name. Ben ignored the glare and moved for Kanigher once more. "She's lead agent with Metcalf gone."

"Really?" Kanigher's arms crossed his chest again, arrogance in his stance.

"Yes. Really." Ben mimicked the man's deep voice. "Morgan should make the call."

Both turned to her. So did everyone else in the room. Adler and Nixon excitedly enjoyed their liquid breakfast and the show on display. Morgan sighed, hands on her hips.

Ben grinned, then rubbed at his neck. "I mean, if she wants to make the call."

The change made sense. Kanigher in charge kept them on the same path. Their relatively brief relationship with the former NSA agent also brought a certain level of doubt that would be detrimental in the field. The team required a fresh start after the expulsion of Metcalf. A clean slate was what the two of them had discussed while locked away.

Morgan cleared her throat. "I want everyone ready to leave for Bismarck in one hour." She spun for the kitchen. "Not you, Nixon. I need you here digging up background data on our target, this signal, and anything else you can find."

"You're benching me and taking the new guy?" Nixon asked.

Morgan glared at him. "The Bunker offers more resources to handle the research side of things. Is that going to be a problem?"

Nixon eyed Holbrook cautiously. The former physician stood innocuously, hands clasped before him as he leaned back and forth along his heels. Slowly, Nixon shook his head and turned to meet Morgan's stern look. "No. No problem at all. I'm your man," Nixon said with a mock salute.

Adler raised her hand slightly. "Zac might not want to come willingly."

"Why not?" Ben asked.

Adler looked down. Morgan approached. "Adler?"

"Kanigher and I caught up with him a while back," she said. "He wasn't..." A stray glance at Kanigher offered her a nod of approval. "There was something wrong with him. I tried to get him to open up, but he—"

"It's okay," Morgan said. Her hand fell on Adler's. "We're going to bring him home."

"Morgan, you didn't see him," Kanigher said. "You don't know what he's even doing in Bismarck, let alone if he wants our help. He might—"

"Can it, Bobby," Morgan snapped. Ben chuckled at the use of the nickname. "Zac is one of us. It's our job to save him, whether it be from Hollis or himself. That's exactly what we're going to do."

CHAPTER SIX

At least the tour went as expected. Quiet awe was the typical response for most of the residents of the Bunker. Holbrook was no exception on that front. He followed Morgan through the kitchen level, down to the training facility, back around to the mainframe, and finally the med-station, which, thankfully, had not been used much.

Questions occasionally blurted out, the usual about the Department of Special Assignments, and the unique history of the group. Morgan did her best to answer, though the doubts of her colleagues preoccupied her thoughts.

What was I thinking? Why did I offer this spot to a total stranger? She knew the truth, of course. She had ruined the man's professional career. No matter the mistakes that preceded his firing, Holbrook didn't deserve to see the end he met, thanks to Morgan's abusive demands. She had given no thought to that consequence. Only Ben's life had mattered, and she'd regretted her thoughtlessness. Offering Holbrook a new home had been the least he deserved for his suffering.

Second chances were the bread and butter of the DSA. Every member of the team, past and present, had made their fair share of errors. Some were bigger than others, Morgan's own, among the top of a long list. Holbrook needed the opportunity to move on from his past, and Morgan was more than willing to give him one.

Everyone else caused doubts to creep up on her. Kanigher especially surprised Morgan. She hoped his anger was nothing more than residual animosity from Metcalf's departure. They continued to reel after their former superior's revelations. Morgan, though, refused to dwell on the woman a moment longer. Division would only break them down, and she needed to build them up.

"Agent Dunleavy?" Holbrook's voice cut through her swirling thoughts and drew her back to the tour.

She shook her head and looked around. Somehow, they had made their way back through the sweeping underground facility and now stood in the dormitory wing. With a deflective smile, Morgan raised her hand to the closed door before them.

"This is you," she announced.

The door opened to the bedroom space. While much better than most of the military bases she'd toured in during her stint overseas, Morgan found the room constricting. The fact they slept under a mountain of soil didn't help matters in her eyes—especially after their recent debacle with Vivian Ness—but she kept the false grin on her face to showcase the room to Holbrook.

He stepped inside and dropped the two suitcases at his sides. A quick sweep of the room showed him the full-size bed along the back wall. To his right was a desk, with a dresser on the opposite wall. A small television sat atop the dresser.

"Bathroom is across the way," Morgan said. "There are clean towels in the breezeway. Laundry machines are down the hall."

Holbrook nodded incessantly. Unable to find any words of his own, silence filled the room. He lifted the suitcases once more and placed them on the bed.

"Right," Morgan muttered. She clapped her hands, then backpedaled for the door. "I'll let you get settled in. We leave in—"

"Agent Dunleavy?" Holbrook said over her.

"Morgan," she replied with a hand over her heart. "Please."

"Morgan." A glimmer of appreciation sat in his eyes. He glanced around the room once more. Sitting along the foot of the bed, he ran his hands over his knees, then looked back at her. The glimmer was gone, replaced by concern. "What am I doing here?"

Morgan couldn't help but chuckle. Holbrook was a smart man. That had been most of the reason for his recruitment: his insightful demeanor.

"Look," she said, pulling the chair out from the desk. She straddled the back of the seat to face him. "I know this wasn't the welcome party you were expecting, or that I was hoping for when I asked you to join. These are good people, though, Simon. They've just been through a lot lately."

Holbrook nodded. "I believe you, and I appreciated the offer when you made it. But I'm not right for this. You have training. You all have specialties that I simply don't. I should go."

He stood. She quickly followed suit and cut him off. "Hold it." Her hand rested on his chest. She patted him lightly, then motioned for him to return to the end of the bed. Simon obliged with a sigh. "You have training, too. Don't deny it. I saw the way you handled your boss. Anne, wasn't it? You called her out and diagnosed that patient correctly, whereas your boss was clueless. Now I don't know why someone with your gift becomes a lab jockey, pushing test tubes all day. That's not my business. But you've got plenty of training, Simon, and we could use you here."

"My point, Morgan, was that you do too," Holbrook said. "Medicine is my life, science, my passion. You're the same — a doctor. So why bring me into this?"

Morgan's gaze fell to the floor. She didn't want to share the truth with him. Thinking of Metcalf, and the unending secrets kept from the team, convinced Morgan otherwise.

"I made a mistake once," she started. "The kind we're not supposed to make. I traded lives, and I can't do that again. I won't."

To save the life of her brother, Morgan had taken medications from three other patients. They had died as a result, all so her brother might live. Their faces continued to haunt her, and would forever. It was a price she had been willing to pay. All it had cost Morgan was her very soul.

"We lost the head of our group recently," Morgan continued. "A long story, and most of it doesn't honestly matter where we're concerned. Now, though, people are looking to me."

Ben's motion for her to lead the team had shocked her. Kanigher was the obvious choice, yet Ben had placed his trust in her. She couldn't do any less for him.

"I can't lead this team and treat their wounds. I can't see them in those two lights at the same time. They blur, and I worry..."

"You might slip again."

Morgan bowed her head. "You helped me before, Simon. I need you to do it again. If you're up for it." She squeezed his shoulder, then let her hand fall away. Soft steps carried her back to the door. "At least give it some thought. We can—"

"Okay."

"Okay?" she asked.

Holbrook stood. "Okay."

A weight left her shoulders with his acceptance. She offered a gracious smile. "Good. Pack a bag. We're rolling in ten."

CHAPTER SEVEN

Zac took a deep breath. His hand rested on the door handle for a minute. He didn't want to be here. His every instinct begged him to wait, to call for help, and then to run as far away from this place as possible. He no longer knew if those feelings came from himself, or the voice in his head.

That thought alone kept him at the door. Being here wasn't a choice—it was the only way to save his life. Saving the future just happened to be a bonus. With nervous sweat pooling down his brow and along his palms, Zac pulled the door open and stepped inside.

The lobby sprawled before him. It covered the entire front half of the building. From there, it branched into corridors that went in multiple directions. To the right and left, there appeared to be offices or maintenance rooms. To the rear, a bank of elevators accessed the rest of the building. A wide staircase sat on the far left to the second level of the lobby, where people milled about against the railing overlooking the entryway.

People packed the place. Some rushed from side to side to various destinations. Receptionists sat in a line to the immediate right of the entry doors. Three women, all smiles, wore headsets while chatting quietly on the phone. What looked to be a tour group waited to the left; their host offered them instructions in boisterous gestures.

At each corner, one to every side of the lobby and at the peak and base of the stairs, stood a plainclothes security officer. The earpieces gave them away to the observant visitor, still standing in the doorway. Security made sense to Zac, yet what surprised him was how sparse it appeared compared to what was being held secret in the building. Surely, something as special as the signal deserved more than a few burly bodyguards at the gate.

The truth came to light quickly for Zac. He saw it in the way stares shot his way the deeper he crept into the lobby. From those pacing above, to the younger members of the tour group, their eyes washed over him in curiosity despite their presence in the building as well.

The movements of those rushing from place to place convinced Zac more was going on. Those that hurried to closing elevators, or whirled around the corners for the offices at the end of the hall, disappeared for a few seconds. Then, like clockwork, they reappeared from a different entry point in the lobby. The elevator personnel returned at the top of the stairs to run the circuit again. The same occurred with those that ducked around corners; they vanished only to reappear at the opposite end of the building, always checking their watches or caught in a conversation with their neighbor that seemed as stuck on repeat as their steps.

"What is this place?" Zac muttered. The sound of his voice caused all movements to cease. Every eye fell on him. Zac reached back for the door, but had stepped too far away to feel the safety of the exit. Each patron of the building, be it employee or guest, stared at Zac. He slowly lifted his hand in a slight wave. "Hi there."

Their heads turned to the right. The attendant at the receptionist's desk grinned from ear to ear. She sat tall and unblinking as Zac followed the silent instructions of the others in the lobby and made his way to the desk.

"Can I help you, sir?" the attendant asked. Her body flinched at his stares. She started to blink her eyes, but the act appeared foreign and forced.

"Maybe?" Zac said. He scanned the room. His cheeks flushed at the constant stares from the others. Leaning over the counter, Zac lowered his voice. "I'm... Well, I'm not really sure what it is I'm looking for exactly, but—"

"Yes, you are," a voice resounded from above.

Zac pushed away from the desk and turned for the far left of the building. A lone woman stood at the landing. All attention gravitated toward her. She wore black pants and a red blouse which billowed around her shoulders as she started down the steps. The shirt matched her lips and brought out the blue of her eyes.

"Excuse me?" Zac moved across the lobby to the bottom of the stairs.

The woman beamed down at him. "Why else would you be here? And now, of all times?"

Heads turned when she passed them, their entire focus locked on her every movement. Zac wished he didn't feel the same. His own body struggled to listen to the growing panic deep in his chest.

The woman stopped short of him. He was forced to look up to catch her eyes; her heels gave her a distinct height advantage. "Welcome, Zachary Modine."

"You know me?"

"Of course," she replied. "It is the Emissary's job to know such things."

"The Emissary?"

She laughed at the question and threw a dismissive wave. "Merely a title. A function, and little else. Like your own as our new Wellspring."

Zac's cheeks burned. He rubbed at the back of his neck. "You know that too, huh?"

The Emissary circled around him. Deep red fingernails ran along his back, but stopped at his shoulder. They dug into him, and she pulled Zac closer. Her smile refused to diminish, and her blue eyes swallowed him whole.

"Come," she said. Her steps carried him along. They journeyed through the lobby. A path widened before them to make way. Zac peered back for the exit—so close, yet completely out of reach. The Emissary gripped tighter and pulled him deeper into the strange building. "I have much to show you, Zachary. Your future awaits."

CHAPTER EIGHT

"You sure this is the place?"

Kanigher rolled his eyes at the question. Ben enjoyed the reaction, especially after repeating himself five times in the last ten minutes. The lack of an answer, however, was far less appealing to the less-than-cordial passenger.

They both sat in a rental van at the corner of Woodbine and Plymouth. Adler's trace pinpointed the precise coordinates for them. Claire confirmed them over the phone. Yet, when both gentlemen looked across the street at the building in question, they doubted the accuracy of their intel.

The building appeared abandoned. Worse, it stood as the most dilapidated, broken-down space within a city mile. The windows along the front had all been shattered, and the brick had slumped along the edifice as if unable to sustain its own weight.

"This is the address," Kanigher said. "Nixon double-checked everything on his end. This is where Zac is."

"And Adler's mystery signal," Ben finished. Two objectives, yet Zac remained the priority. Ben tried not to let it bother him, not to hear Morgan's concern for their onetime colleague. *Like that had been the end of his connection to Morgan.* Ben grumbled under his breath, then unclasped his seatbelt. He opened the door.

"I'm going to check it out."

"Check what out?" Kanigher asked. "The place is an eyesore. No one here will even look at it."

Ben scanned the block. Kanigher was right. Not one person made eye contact with the space at the corner. If they were glancing in that direction prior to reaching the building, their heads immediately shot down to their feet or ahead to the next block. Most stopped all movement, and either turned around, or jaywalked to the opposite side of the street.

"Weird," Ben muttered. "So, why are we different?"

Kanigher ran his hand under his chin. "Not sure. Possibly because of the trace we ran?"

"So because we know the place exists, we can look at it?"

"Sounds plausible enough," Kanigher commented. "I guess."

"See, Kanigher? Confidence like that is why you didn't win the leadership role." Ben pushed off the van and started across the street.

"Yeah, well, I think Morgan could use my skill-set more than yours." Anger sat in his voice over their earlier argument. Ben hadn't meant to broach the topic again, but his brain and mouth no longer agreed on much.

"Probably." Ben rushed across the street before the light changed. He stood at the corner, hands to his lips to carry the sound back to his colleague. "Though I do bring a certain enjoyment to the workplace."

"Aggravation is more like it," Kanigher shouted back. "Now hurry up. This place gives me the creeps."

It was another fair assessment. The second Ben started toward the building, he felt resistance from his body. His legs cramped up slightly, and his heart pounded in his chest. Sweat dotted his brow and soaked his shirt like an early-warning system from his body. Something was off about the place. Ben stopped at the sidewalk and peered back at the waiting van.

"Well?" Kanigher asked. "What are you waiting for?"

Ben gazed down at his heavy feet, weighed down by irrational fear. He tried to pry his legs loose from the pavement, as if stuck in wet cement, yet failed to budge from the spot.

"Riley?"

"I can honestly say, Kanigher, I have no idea what's wrong with me at this moment."

"Do you need me to—"

Ben shook his head. "No. I've got this."

"Do you?"

"I do," Ben answered.

He spun to face the dilapidated structure. He lifted his right leg, fighting through the sudden weight of the limb, and edged away from the sidewalk for the waiting structure. A breath of relief left him from the exertion. He did the same with the left. Free from the sidewalk, Ben grinned at Kanigher, who continued to stare in bewilderment at Ben's actions.

"Hurry it up!"

Ben waved down the cry. Each step toward the building was agony. Fear threatened to topple him with every inch gained, but Ben refused to be stopped. Fighting through the pain in his legs and the tightness in his chest, Ben pushed closer and closer to the building.

When his hand touched the handle of the cracked entry door, all trace of the fear vanished. The pain left him, and he wondered if it had all been in his head or not. He turned toward Kanigher, who offered a slight shrug of confusion. Ben offered the same, then opened the door.

Inside, the lobby sprawled before him. Dozens of people rushed across the area. All signs of the broken-down husk of a structure were gone, instantly replaced with a gleaming office. The sounds of murmured conversations and ringing phones filled his ears.

Ben took a step back. The door closed at his exit. He peered up, prepared to view the slumped brick and the broken windows of the building. Instead, a silver spire rose into the sky. Impossible curves adorned the edifice, a metallic shine to the entire place that left it completely unique to the surrounding architecture.

"What the hell?"

Ben back-pedaled to the curb. The spire remained, where once it had been hidden from view.

"Well?" Kanigher called.

"This is definitely the place," Ben yelled, unable to stop staring. A hand waved Kanigher over. "See for yourself."

Kanigher made his way across the street. "This another of your jokes?"

"I wish," Ben said, his jaw barely able to close—still in awe at the structure's change. "Open the door. You'll see."

Kanigher started ahead. A grunt escaped him, and Ben stopped his gaping stare at the building to witness Kanigher's struggle toward the door.

"I don't think anything's here," Kanigher said. He turned for their van.

Ben shook his head. "Push through it. It's right there. You just have to push through it."

"I've never felt this before," Kanigher said. "It's like my entire body is fighting me."

"It is. Don't let it win."

Kanigher snarled. Every step caused him to wince with intense pain, but he continued on past Ben for the building. He snatched the door handle with both hands. Breath returned to him. "Unbelievable."

"Say that again after you open the door."

Kanigher ducked his head inside the building. A second later, he returned, his eyes wider than Ben had ever seen them before. "H—How?" the man stuttered. "How is it possible? How do you hide a building?"

"I wish I knew," Ben said. Kanigher joined him at the curb to stare up the length of the spire. "A better question might be, *why* do you hide a building?"

"That's just the first line of defense." Kanigher pointed through the windows that ran the length of the lobby. "Security is all over the place in there. There's something off about the other people, too."

Ben tilted his head to the street. "Let's not draw too much attention our way."

"Good idea."

They returned to the van, hopped inside, and slammed the doors shut behind them. Ben scanned the front of the building. Pedestrians continued to avoid eye contact with the place. They skirted around the entire property to avoid the same bone-chilling fear that had taken over both agents.

Ben slowly noticed the level of security within the mysterious structure. The plainclothes guards were easy to spot; they made little effort to blend in with the crowd wandering both levels of the lobby. Each guard had a shoulder-holster and together monitored every sight line within the space.

Kanigher's tactical mind was as sharp as ever, something Ben had trouble giving the man credit for. It reminded him of the earlier argument over leadership and his own hand in the confrontation.

"Listen, Kanigher, I..." Ben paused. He ran a hand through his hair, then settled along the sill of the window. "I'm sorry about before."

"It's fine, Riley," Kanigher said. "It's been a rough week."

"No excuse," Ben replied. "I thought you were here to sabotage us, and I've treated you like garbage more often than not. I was wrong."

Ben extended his hand. Kanigher's eyebrow rose. "Really?"

"Take the hand, man."

"No joy buzzer?"

"Left it in my duffel bag."

"Poor guy," Kanigher said with a laugh. He shook the hand. "So what's our move?"

Kanigher stared at the lobby. "I think they'll stonewall us in there." He pointed down to the corner of the building, and another entry point—this time a solid metal door with no view of the inside. "Alarms will sound with any emergency exit on the ground."

"Leaving us the air," Ben said. "And me without my jetpack."

Kanigher looked up. "I know a guy in the area that can help with that."

"Of course you do." It was another knee-jerk reaction to the man's commitment to the team. Ben rolled his eyes. "Sorry."

"No problem," Kanigher said. "I'm used to your foot resting in your mouth."

"It is the style these days."

Kanigher turned the key in the ignition and brought the van to life. "Let's head back and tell Morgan what we've found." He waited for traffic to clear before he turned around for the far side of the road. The van jerked steadily, then settled as they started away from the building. "We're fighting the clock on this one."

"Aren't we always?"

"Yeah." Kanigher glimpsed the building in the rearview mirror. "But I've got a feeling time is running out quickly."

Ben wished he could disagree. He wanted to tell Kanigher that he was wrong, that things would work out. Ben, however, had felt the same damn thing the second they'd arrived.

CHAPTER NINE

Kanigher waited until the door closed behind Ben, and the small alleyway to the rear of the team's makeshift safe house was clear. He hated keeping the secret from Ben, especially after their heart-to-heart. It had taken them too long to come together as a team.

The call to his friend went quickly. There was shorthand with friends, like a latent telepathic link that redefined the need to verbalize every intention. With the extra time afforded him thanks to his friend's quick acceptance of the task, Kanigher stared at the contact list on his phone. It was relatively bare. His brother took the top spot—only his first name to keep it as secure as possible in case he lost the device. The same paranoia held true for every contact, including the one his thumb hovered over. He simply listed her using the letter S.

He hesitated to make the call. The urge had hit him the second he'd noticed her missing. Now, it had been days without a word. The team wanted nothing to do with her. Part of him still felt slighted at the secrets kept—yet there was a fine line between being miffed and writing off someone entirely.

His thumb pressed hard on the screen, and the call connected. It rang twice, then clicked over. Silence dominated the line. Kanigher fought the urge to speak. He recognized the game being played on the other end; she always loved to control everything.

"Do they know you're calling me?" Susan Metcalf finally said.

"No." Despite the empty alley, Kanigher sank deeper into his seat. The phone tucked tight to his shoulder, almost hidden from view. "I told them I was reaching out to an old buddy. Not a lie. Just didn't take that long to make the arrangements."

"Anyone I know?"

"You might say that," Kanigher said with a laugh. "You remember Davey?"

Metcalf groaned. His smile widened at the reaction. There was no surprise at her disgust. Her initial experience with the man had not gone well, to say the least. "You mean that moron pilot friend of yours? I almost jumped out of the plane to get away from him. Without a chute."

It was a good memory, one of many the two shared. They had taken the trip to escape from responsibilities and obligations. Metcalf had been hip deep in forming the DSA, working with the burgeoning Inter-Agency Council for approvals on everything from personnel to paperclips.

Kanigher had offered a break. When Grissom had bowed out at the last minute, Kanigher had been even more excited about the quiet diversion from reality. It had been a chance to spend some time alone with Metcalf, who had never looked past Grissom to truly see Kanigher in any way other than a colleague. He had hoped the trip might change her outlook.

Davey had volunteered to fly them out to the resort. Kanigher had taken the opportunity to relax and hoped Metcalf might follow suit. What he had failed to realize had been Metcalf's idea of relaxation merely meant working while ten thousand feet in the air.

She had used the trip for her own needs—to track down a lead on the Wellspring. The lead had failed to pan out, and the trip had been nothing but a large circle from airport to airport for a quick return. Davey had laughed his ass off over Kanigher's luck.

Kanigher, however, had felt nothing but rejection. His anger had carried through the weeks and months that followed, yet faded as time passed until his own laughter joined Davey's when reminiscing about the trip. He could hardly blame Metcalf for his hidden agenda. What their trip made him realize was how dedicated the woman had always been. For Susan, only the mission mattered.

"Yeah, well, Davey's local, and we need him."

"How bad is it?" she asked, concern in her voice. He wondered if it was for him, but knew the truth centered on the team as a whole.

"Too many unknowns," he said. "Including your boy, Zac. I don't like it, but I don't have to. If we can save him…"

"You will."

Kanigher huffed. He sat up taller and cradled the phone. "I was calling to check on you, not to offer a briefing. Where are you?"

"Following up on a lead," she replied. He heard pelting rain on a windshield through the line. Tires squealed in the background. "I'm fine, Bobby."

"Yeah right," Kanigher said. "How deep in it are you?"

"I have it covered," Metcalf answered. "You keep our people safe your way, and I'll do it mine."

"Why do you think I'm calling?" he said. "That attitude is what worries me most about you out there on your own."

Brakes rang out. The sound of tires bumping off the road was loud and clear through the line.

"Susan?"

"I have to go, Bobby. Keep in touch."

"Wait," Kanigher called. "Sus—"

The line went dead. Kanigher pulled the phone away and stared at the screen. He closed his eyes, then dropped the device in his lap.

"So much for making me feel better."

He hoped the call might help bring him relief over her swift departure. They had yet to talk about the decision made by the team whether to allow her to stay on with the DSA or not. The truth was, the decision mattered little to the woman. Metcalf made her own decisions, and everyone else had to live with them, whether they liked them or not.

She frustrated him like no other, yet captivated him for the same reasons. He missed her. Despite the secrets and the lies that divided them, Kanigher believed they could have moved past them all and made things work.

Keep in touch. Her last words rang in his every thought. Kanigher picked up the phone and slipped it in his pocket. Opening the van door, he started for the safe house.

"Yeah, I'll keep in touch," he muttered to himself. "Only because I know you won't."

CHAPTER TEN

Metcalf turned off her phone and set it in the center console before closing up the compartment. She exited the vehicle with haste. Her hands delicately placed the door back into the frame with a soft click.

She had parked deep in a wooded area outside a suburb in Western Pennsylvania. Light traffic traveled the road, the street a veritable forest compared to the bustle of the major thorough-fares less than three miles north. The black sedan hid nicely among the brush, unable to be seen from the street.

The ride had been bought and paid for out of her pocket. A local kid who'd needed beer money had been more than willing to take the cash deal when offered. She'd customized it herself over the course of the previous day. She replaced the muffler to ensure the quietest drive possible and also added compartments throughout for her equipment.

Slipping deeper into the woods, Metcalf brought her sniper rifle to bear. She stayed low to the ground, shuffling through the wet leaves left by the long winter. They no longer crunched, but slid away with her every step.

At the perimeter of the property, Metcalf slowed. Along the tree line, she noticed several motion sensors. Staggered along the way, they left few gaps in the field. Paranoia was the hallmark of the man inside the estate—a man with more than a few secrets. Metcalf required those secrets. They were the reason for her visit on the gray, rain-filled afternoon.

Careful to stick close to the trees, Metcalf shimmied up the nearest trunk. Her fingers deftly detached the sensor from its base, then quickly turned it off before it transmitted the shift to the security force within the estate.

She followed the same routine twice more. That was more than enough to give her a clear route onto the property. Cameras might have worked better, offering picture to go along with the sensor, but motion sensors were much more economical so far from the power grid.

It was yet another mark of the man, and something he would come to regret.

The cameras didn't come into play until she reached the wall surrounding the manor. They cycled ninety-degrees in an arc. Their rotations were timed to keep most of the forest in sight— but never the totality, which was impossible with the amount of land to cover.

Metcalf waited for the cameras to finish their latest sweep. She prepared her gear, including a grapple for the top of the wall. Her rifle hugged her back. Careful breaths calmed her body. As the cameras started their shift, Metcalf made her approach. She crept along the ground; her black outfit gave her the best cover available. Close enough to the wall, she jumped to her feet and slipped into the shadows afforded by the ten-foot tall brick barricade.

Another rotation started. Metcalf carefully backed away from the wall. Swinging the grapple rope, she launched the hook toward the peak. It caught along the brick, and she pulled it taut until the line was completely secure. Once more, Metcalf tucked close to the wall. Long breaths and closed eyes kept her calm through the rest of the rotation.

With the start of the third camera shift, Metcalf began her climb. She made no noise and used the wall for support to pull herself up. Reaching the top, Metcalf immediately removed the grapple. Hugging the wall close, she jumped down to the estate proper.

The manor lay in the distance, insignificant compared to the rest of the property. The grounds were more extensive within the barricade than without. Everything inside the walls of the estate was perfectly maintained. Trees were present, though each was trimmed and well-kept. Bare hillsides ran along the western front, with a converted golf course immaculately revitalized since the recently ended winter season. Flower gardens towered along the south, a barrier from the soaring slices and stray golf balls.

Metcalf left the safety of the wall. Huddling close to the ground, she reached the edge of the hill before her. At the top, she halted and removed her rifle. Careful to position it, Metcalf set up the delicate instrument, then peered through the scope.

Security roamed the manor in packs. While technology covered the perimeter, personnel secured the inner sanctum of their boss. Breaching the palatial domicile was a dangerous move, even in the best of circumstances. There was too much ground to cover. A team was necessary for a precision operation of this magnitude, the very thing Metcalf had lost.

The sniper rifle was the best option for the moment. It had always been her favorite recon tool, and she held it like an old friend. Turning away from the security outside the home, Metcalf scanned each open window for signs of life within.

On the second-floor balcony, she found her man: Malcolm Richards. Richards was a political insider of the highest order. His lobby group had been the primary sponsor of several high-profile bills on the House floor in the last year. She couldn't care less about his political influence, or what hands the man had greased to get to where he was in life. Metcalf had trailed him for only one reason.

He had been at Sebastian Duloc's party in New York—the private celebration in the penthouse suite. Those downstairs had been present for a night of drinks and dancing, while the penthouse had been reserved for only the most special of guests. Each one was part of a secret group with controlling interests in every major field of study. Richards had been among them, and his attendance marked him as a member of the Trust.

Metcalf pulled the trigger, the safety still in place. It was nice practice for what she had planned for the man at the end of the scope. Richards was well-connected, and an insider in the Trust. She had need of both aspects. For her team's safety, and for the mission ahead, it was time to have a heart-to-heart with Malcolm Richards.

CHAPTER ELEVEN

Morgan tried to relax. She paced the small room on the second floor of the safe house. The floorboards creaked under her weight. Nerves jangled beneath the skin. Waves of anxiety shot up her arms and down her legs, then back up through her chest, where they sat like a pit in her gut. Morgan wanted to scream. Worse, she wanted to crawl right out of her skin, jump from the window, and run away from every responsibility thrust upon her with this mission.

She couldn't stop worrying about Zac. It had been too long since their last conversation—one that had not gone well. She'd pushed him away, angry and afraid of the choices he had made in what she now realized had been an impossible situation. Sullivan had manipulated Zac, suckered him into turning on the team for the sake of his family and his career. Morgan hadn't seen it as anything other than a betrayal before. Now, with him so close—and in terrible danger—all her anger at Zac's behavior faded behind concern.

The concern, though, merely added to the pressure of the mission. Was this how Metcalf felt with every case thrown their way? Was the pressure of leading the team what caused her to close off so completely—to push everyone else away rather than display any vulnerability?

Morgan hated to sympathize with the woman. After everything Metcalf had hidden from them, from the lies that accompanied almost every single mission the team had handled from its inception, Morgan wanted nothing to do with her former superior. Yet right now, the urge to throw up from the weight of the leadership role threatened to overwhelm her.

The past haunted Morgan. Decisions she'd made to save her brother's life circled back on her with every rotation around the room. Ben pushed for her to take charge. Instinct agreed with that sentiment, but staring at the situation ahead of them left Morgan cursing the many variables that made their cause so unpredictable.

Lives were at stake, and it was her job to save them the best way she could. The team required her guidance to hold them together.

Morgan took a sharp breath, then left the room behind. A quick jaunt down the stairs brought her to the first floor. The others waited patiently. Kanigher stood at the window overlooking the street. Ben packed up the vehicles in the neighboring garage—visible through the open layout of the space. Holbrook and Adler sat around a table left behind by the previous tenants. Adler tapped away at the tablet locked in her grip. Holbrook, the newcomer to the party, simply waited. His eyes struggled against the urge for a mid-afternoon nap.

All distractions ended upon her arrival. Their concerns melded with her own. She swallowed them down. She refused to allow her doubts to win.

"Okay, people," she announced. "Here's what we're going to do."

Ben closed the door to the secondary sedan parked next to the team's van. They'd procured the vehicle for the same reason they'd taken up residence in the abandoned warehouse in the heart of Bismarck: to stay close to the situation while maintaining the ability to move at a moment's notice. He left behind the packing to return to the room with the rest of the team.

"What's the play, boss?" Ben said upon entering. Morgan sent a blistering glare back his way. She didn't need the reminder of her new role.

She focused on the rest of the team, rather than fall for Ben's puppy-dog look of apology. "Ben and I are running point on this. We go in through the roof, which Nixon has been able to pinpoint through whatever strange camouflage is going on with the building. We get in, locate Zac, and get the hell out of there. That's our primary objective. Bringing home one of our own."

Adler raised a hand. "What about—"

"Getting there, Adler." Morgan cut her off. The signal had

been Adler's only concern since the implosion at the Cove. Every waking moment of the woman's life had been spent to track it down, to learn all she could about what it contained. To Adler, the signal was her Holy Grail. Morgan's view, however, differed greatly. "The signal is secondary."

"What?" Adler nearly tumbled from her chair in shock. The reaction was unusual for the typically reserved analyst. "You can't be serious. After all the time I've spent on this. I need to—"

"That's the way it is," Morgan said. Adler quieted, sinking in her chair. "Alison, I want the truth as much as you. However, we both know Hollis and his goons won't be far behind, if they aren't here already. Learning everything we can about what is going on inside that structure is *our* secondary objective. But it's *your* first. From here."

"How? I—"

"Ben and I will be wired for sound and audio," Morgan continued. "We will feed you live telemetry the entire time we're onsite."

Adler hesitated. She wanted more.

Morgan leaned close. "You will find your answers, Adler. I promise."

Kanigher shook his head. "I should be with you. You're going to need me."

"I do need you, Kanigher. Here. With Adler and Holbrook."

"Morgan," Kanigher said in a sharp tone. "All due respect, but we're talking about my intel and my pilot."

"And I appreciate both," Morgan shot back quickly. She didn't need the power struggle, or another fight on her hands. "You're staying. End of discussion."

Silence fell between them. Even Ben managed to keep his trap shut for a few seconds, the urge for a witty comment clear from his bulging eyes. Out of everyone, it was Holbrook who broke the quiet of the warehouse. His hand slowly raised, as if in school. Morgan nodded to him in answer.

"Everyone has been nice enough not to ask, so I will," he said. "Why am I here?"

"I wasn't going to ask," Ben said. Relief filled his face. While she appreciated his restraint, her partner remained little more than a petulant child who needed to make noise whenever possible. "Okay, I was going to ask. His way was nicer."

"Ben…"

He took a step away from the group. "I'm done. Don't mind me."

"Never do," Morgan grumbled. She turned to Holbrook. "Simon, Zac may require medical attention, and your expertise may come in handy." She peered around the room. "Everyone good with that answer?"

They offered appreciative nods. Ben gave her a thumbs up. "Peachy."

"Great," she said, hands tight along the edge of the table. "I don't like this situation any more than you do. This isn't for us. We're not here to satisfy our curiosity or solve the mystery of the universe. We're here for Zac. Now let's go get him."

CHAPTER TWELVE

The moment the plane touched down at Bismarck Airport, Hollis moved for the door to disembark. A headache plagued him, residual pain from his morning meeting. The complaints of lesser beings who refused to know their place in the world always bothered him. Didn't they realize the importance of the Trust? His work alone helped change the world, yet if the slightest bit of bad press floated in their general direction, panic ensued.

The Trust was meant for more than that. Humanity deserved to rise above its pettiness and achieve wonders, yet dollar signs and profit margins continued to stand in their way. They worried about their quarterly earnings and how their companies were trading overseas, rather than see the larger picture.

Hollis never had that issue. He always knew the road ahead would be long, but so very rewarding. The work he had done from a young age was nothing less than the culmination of a dream—his dream.

Whenever someone tried to step on that dream, whenever the peons cried foul play or stamped their feet in protest, Hollis felt the road stretch out further into the distance, and his goals fall out of reach. Irritation rewarded his hard work, and he tired of the fight with those undeserving twits.

Personnel scattered from him as he left the plane. They tried to offer reports and status updates. He took them in hand, but cared little at the moment. All that mattered to Hollis was Zac's current position, and what secrets they might find.

A car waited for Hollis on the tarmac. He straightened the collar of his tan jacket, then proceeded to the back seat. Slipping inside, he let out a long, calming breath. His back settled into the cushion, and relief washed over him.

"How was your flight?"

Hollis barely made out the figure through the shadows of the cabin. Just her presence forced a grin to his lips. "Abysmal," he said. "Not a surprise, considering my morning. So why don't you brighten my spirits?"

The woman smirked devilishly at him. His hand reached for her, but found a tablet waiting for him. "Our tracer went dead, but not before we pinpointed Modine's last location."

Hollis scanned the topographical map on the display. A single dot illuminated a downtown intersection. "What am I looking at here?"

"A curiosity like I've never seen," the woman replied. Her hair covered her eyes as she bent over the computer. She swiped a single finger across the screen. The map image changed to a visual of the building in question. The place appeared abandoned, with shattered windows and cracked edifice.

"This is not what I was expecting." Hollis had imagined wonders, not commonplace trash. His headache increased, and with it, the pressure he placed on the corner of the fragile device. "This isn't—"

"The truth," the woman interjected.

"Pardon me?"

"Walk up to the corner of Woodbine and Plymouth, and you will find this building," she said. "Everything about it screams to be ignored, to turn away for someplace better, to go anywhere else but here. Except this image is false."

"It is?"

She nodded. "It took three of our people to even reach the building. The first two made it ten steps before turning away, like their bodies refused to go near the place. The third, however, pushed through the field. This is what he saw, and we've been able to see the same ever since."

The woman swiped the screen once more. The dilapidated building vanished from view. In its place, a gleaming tower of silver stood arcing up into the Bismarck skyline. The metal used along the exterior appeared to absorb the natural light of the world, bending it to suit the structure's needs.

"Incredible." Hollis zoomed in on the image. The building

defied every architectural law. Curves dominated the structure instead of straight angles. Even the windows seemed to be made of a glass he didn't recognize. "Simply incredible."

The woman's excitement grew. "I agree."

"Any idea who owns the building?"

"None," she said. "It certainly isn't one of ours. There are no identifying marks along the exterior. No liens or leases, or any other document at the County Clerk's office. There is no record of this building existing, let alone who occupies it currently."

"There wouldn't be," Hollis said. "It's theirs."

For as long as Hollis had known the Wellspring, he'd always suspected there had been more to her, and her story. The Cove should have been the first clue to a greater secret, yet all Hollis had seen at the time was opportunity—for himself and for the Trust. She had claimed to have constructed the underground lab, and he had never questioned the legitimacy of that claim.

The Wellspring had offered the future, but where had the information come from exactly? This was it: the home of the true puppet masters behind the Wellspring and where the future was truly born.

"Sir?"

Hollis passed her the tablet, then sank into his seat. "Were you ever able to visit the Cove?"

"No, sir."

He cocked an eyebrow toward her, surprised to hear her answer. A quick recall reminded him of how recently the woman had joined his team. Her advancement had come quickly, thanks to her ability and determination. She was the most remarkable investigator Hollis had seen in a generation, with an eye toward the larger picture he so cherished. Hollis was glad to have her by his side now. He needed people he could trust.

"That building, the true building, has the same architectural design elements," Hollis said. "That same unique metal, the use of curves and arches. It doesn't match anything else in the world."

"Yet the Trust was unaware of this asset?"

Hollis nodded slowly. "Which means the Wellspring hid this from us. And who knows what else?"

This had always been his concern: that the benevolence of the Wellspring was a feint. While they used her knowledge for their own betterment—both monetarily and to increase their influence—she worked for a completely separate goal. Hollis refused to jeopardize the Trust's work. Humanity had come too far as a species in the last century to be waylaid by outside interests.

"What resources do we have?"

"Two squads," the woman said. "They've been dispatched as ordered, and will be here within the hour."

"Have them meet us onsite," Hollis said. "I'll be leading the first team through the building myself."

"Sir?" Her brow furrowed. She leaned closer, and the shadows lifted from her delicate skin. "I don't believe that's a prudent course of action. We don't know what is inside. The threat—"

"Will be negligible with a full team of armed soldiers, don't you think?"

She took a long breath. "Why take the risk when I can easily handle this?"

"You'll be busy with the second team."

"Objective?"

"The DSA," Hollis answered. "Metcalf and her cronies won't be far behind us. Hell, they're probably already here. Find their base of operations. Apprehend only. I want them out of our way, not dead. Not yet, anyway."

"I see." She fell back into her seat. The darkness swallowed her features, but he caught her eyes staring out toward the city.

"Will that be a problem for you?" Hollis asked.

It was another test, one she passed when her lips curled and her gaze fell on him once more. "Not at all, sir. Not at all."

CHAPTER THIRTEEN

The Emissary escorted Zac around every floor in the strange, wondrous complex. She didn't push, didn't prod, and never mentioned the work being accomplished. The hard sell wasn't necessary; the work spoke for itself.

Entire floors were dedicated to laboratories that held equipment Zac had never seen before. From the manufacturing of sophisticated robotics, to the processing of new plastics with a tensile strength that surpassed the shells of satellites, Zac marveled with every turn and every step through the building.

Some labs ran three or four floors up with decking around the periphery, and thin, metal stairwells for access to each station throughout. People monitored the progress within, though at a closer inspection Zac wondered if *people* was even the correct term. They stood glassy-eyed and motionless, like those in the lobby, like they were lost to a task instead of seeing the world around them. The presence of a stranger among them jarred no reaction. Each one stared blankly, either at a machine or a screen. They made no notes and offered no input to the process.

Floors passed by in a blur. Zac tried to keep up with the Emissary, yet became lost to the various processes contained throughout the complex. What was the purpose behind each one? What was being developed here that needed to be kept secret from the outside world? And what did it mean for him? Many more questions passed through his whirling thoughts until he finally came to a halt outside a smaller diagnostic room.

Inside, small chips were being sorted and cataloged. Mechanical arms handled the task. Multiple rows occupied the space, and within each one a different configuration of chip. The arms set them in the correct sequence, where they were sent down a conveyor belt. The chips then became embedded into a patch of white. After the embedding, the patches found their way into a final batch and stacked for later shipping.

Zac shook his head, unable to understand the item being produced. The voice in his head stayed unusually quiet as well, though he felt a wave of anxiety rising from the Wellspring.

The Emissary waited at the end of the corridor, ready for the next level of their tour. Zac stopped and pointed inside the lab. "I don't recognize any of this." The woman in the red blouse and dark pants cocked her head toward him, then turned to approach. Zac continued to stare into the lab, a hand to the back of his neck. "Now, I'm not saying I'm anywhere close to a genius with innovative technology, but I would have hoped to figure out something from all these machines and labs you have in here. Yet, I still don't have a clue about anything you're doing."

"That surprises me, Zachary," the Emissary said. Her eyes flashed before him, like a scanner washing over his body. "I've been aware of your presence since you left Maine some time ago. I would have expected the Wellspring to have informed you of everything long before your arrival."

"Ha."

The Emissary's head tilted with curiosity at his reaction. She did not know the agony Zac had faced in suppressing the Wellspring. He could still feel the pain bubbling beneath the surface, his memories in flux as the protocol threatened to subsume his very identity. When it came to actually being informed by the system, though, Zac had found the Wellspring to be less than forthcoming.

Zac waved the Emissary ahead. She offered an awkward shrug of dismissal before heading back toward the stairs and the continuation of their tour. Zac, however, remained before the narrow window into the lab. His reflection slowly faded behind the face of another: April Newton.

"What was so funny, Zac?"

He chuckled at her indignant tone. "The idea that you inform me of anything."

"Replace inform with take over, and you get the Emissary's true meaning." April shot a glare at the woman by the stairs. "So, you're welcome."

"Yeah, well, you have been trying your best," Zac said. "I don't think a thank you is in order."

"It's inevitable, Zac," she replied. "It's either the protocol, or death. As long as the signal is in place. Destroy it and—"

"I go free," Zac interrupted, the song and dance well known to him. "Free to be with..."

The name disappeared. He had carried it with him for so long, yet struggled to lock it in place. There was no sign of the knowledge. Panic set in. Zac shut his eyes tight. He tried to picture a face—something to help him remember. Nothing but darkness greeted his frantic thoughts.

"Claire," April said.

The second she spoke the name, Zac opened his eyes. Clarity returned, and with it everything that threatened to slip away. Claire and Alex. His time at the DSA with Morgan, Ben, and Metcalf. Each name returned as quickly as they'd vanished.

"I know," he lied. Zac padded his forehead clear of sweat. He felt feverish and ill. His body fought to reject the protocol, but how much longer that fight would last was in question—like so many other things in his life.

"Zachary?" the Emissary called from the stairs.

Zac watched the visage of April fade and his reflection took over. The image was just as much a stranger as the woman locked in his brain. The world slipped away from him.

"Coming," he said. "Sorry."

"It's a lot to take in," the Emissary said with a smile.

Zac nodded, then joined her at the stairs for the next level. "It is. But I have to ask. What's the point of it all?"

"To protect the signal at the heart of the complex, of course," she answered. "That's why you came, isn't it? For your instructions from the chamber?"

Zac hesitated. She turned to face him. Her curiosity bordered on annoyance. Zac grinned anxiously, unsure how to reply. He had no knowledge of this place, or his role in it. Not to the extent she believed, at any rate.

"Yeah," Zac said. "Of course, that's why I'm here."

"Wonderful." The Emissary cast all doubt from her face and continued their ascent. "The signal is the key to the future. It is our guide to distribute to humanity so they can prepare the path for the future. So we may welcome the arrival of the First with open arms and glad hearts."

"The First?" Zac muttered. No one had ever mentioned anything about any *First* before. The first of what, exactly? "What's—"

"Come, Zachary," the Emissary interjected. Her steps hastened, pulling him forward toward the end of his journey. "You have questions. The Signal Chamber holds all your answers."

CHAPTER FOURTEEN

Ben sensed Morgan's unease the entire drive to the airfield. There were no jokes about who would drive, and she displayed none of the confidence typical for the daytime jaunt. Her new role was the culprit, therefore Ben held the blame.

She was the right person for the job. He had seen it multiple times in their work. Each case brought out her leadership qualities—the way she organized and motivated those around her, including any local law enforcement caught in the middle of their usual insanity.

Yet, since assuming the reins from Metcalf, Morgan had become too inflexible about the team dynamic. Sure, Kanigher needed to be put in his place—one of Ben's favorite pastimes, which he swore never to do again now that they were *besties*— but the man had brought up plenty of good points. They relied on Kanigher's intel, and his contact, to infiltrate the mysterious downtown structure. Kanigher's help might have gone a long way to making the mission a surefire success.

Instead, Morgan had cut him off at the knees and put everything on her shoulders. She brought Ben along just for his looks, or so he assumed, with the way the wind blew his hair perfectly off his face.

Reality sank in for Ben when they reached the airfield. He shook away the juvenile theatrics in order to win a smile from his closed-off partner. Rather than try to annoy her into speaking, he decided a more subtle approach was warranted.

"So," he said, drawing out the word. "I thought the briefing went well."

Morgan slammed the car door shut behind her, a groan on

her lips. He might have been better off with the juvenile theatrics.

"I'm not interested in your analysis." Morgan started out on the tarmac. Small planes were pulled from their bays, some for use and others for routine maintenance. No one gave the pair of agents a passing look once they made it past the gate and the armed security manning the post.

"You are, though," Ben said as he caught up to her. "Come on, Morgan. You're tense. You're stressed. Neither will help get Zac back. That's what you want, isn't it?"

"Of course, that's what I..." Her whole body ground to a halt. In that moment, Ben saw the truth in her face. Morgan was conflicted about the operation, not because of what they were doing, but who they were doing it for. She still loved him, even though he had sided with Sullivan. Morgan shook her head. "I want Zac safe, Ben. That's all."

He wanted to believe her, wished with all his heart that had been the truth of the matter. Her wide eyes told a different tale. Ben fell back on his heels, hands in his pockets. "Yeah, of course," he said. "So do I. The team feels the same way. We just need you to trust in us."

"I do."

"Morgan..."

"I do, Ben," she repeated in a huff. "I do, it's... never mind."

Ben held her up with his hand. "No way. Let's air this out now instead of our usual waiting until the bullets are flying shtick."

"I thought you preferred it that way," she said with a smirk.

"Oh, definitely," Ben chided. "Mixing it up keeps us fresh, though. It keeps us young."

Morgan shook her head, then pushed past him. "See, now I thought that was why you still wear Spider-Man pajamas."

Ben laughed. "You can't distract me with witty charm, Agent Dunleavy."

She sighed. "I do trust in the team, Ben. It's me I have a problem with."

"Then let it go," Ben said. "Because I'd trust you with my life."

"Thanks, I..." Morgan looked off into the distance. Recognition filled her face. "That must be him."

The helicopter rested on the pad, ready for flight. Gear was packed into the rear. The door was opened, and a man wearing jeans and a bright Hawaiian shirt went through what appeared to be his pre-flight checklist.

This is as close to Oahu as I'm getting in this lifetime, Ben thought as they approached the man and his fashionable shirt.

The man tossed the list inside to greet them. His thick white hair was tied off in the back. His skin was tanned despite the early days of summer still a month away.

"You must be the lucky couple on their honeymoon." The man held his hand out to Ben.

Morgan took the gesture, which surprised the man. "No, we're not—"

The pilot smiled while he shook. "Bobby recommended me, of all folks, for the job. Kind of the man, considering our history. Name's Davey."

"An adult willing to go with Davey?" Ben commented. "Yeah, this should turn out well."

Morgan slapped Ben's arm. "Ignore him."

Davey nodded. "No choice." He tapped his left ear where Ben stood closest. "Deaf on that side."

Ben rolled his eyes. "Even better."

"I did hear that one."

Morgan smiled. She lifted her gear for the man, who stowed it away in the cabin. "Kanigher bring you up to speed?"

Davey helped her inside, then assisted Ben. "On your little sightseeing tour of our fair city? Yes indeed, ma'am."

"Let's forgo the ma'am talk for all our sanity," Morgan said. "And we're not the sightseeing type."

"I figured," Davey said with a wink. He closed the door and climbed into position behind the stick.

Morgan leaned close. "Now, we're not sure what we'll find at the site, but if you can—"

"I'll stop you there," Davey said. "The less I know, the better. Bobby says you need a lift? I aim to please. No questions asked. That way, when it hits the fan, like it always does, no one is putting the blame on the poor, ignorant pilot."

"Smart."

"Momma didn't raise no dummy, and poppa never raised no liar," Davey said. "I'll get you where you're going."

"Much appreciated," Morgan said. "We're ready when you are."

"Who wouldn't be on a beautiful day like this?" Davey started the engine. The propeller whirled overhead, and the noise filled the cabin. With each rotation, Davey's grin widened. "Bismarck awaits. Buckle up."

They settled into their seats. Neither one relaxed, though. Their nerves kept them on high alert. They were on their way. Their plan had come together smoothly for a change. That fact failed to make either of them feel any better about what lay ahead.

CHAPTER FIFTEEN

Trucks lined the block leading to Woodbine. Another row of supply vans and personnel transports parked along the cross street. The Trust had secured the entire area in a matter of minutes. The two teams poured into the zone at a breakneck pace.

Several officers took up positions at every intersection surrounding the zone. They diverted traffic away from the corner. Pedestrians were told to vacate the block, excuses offered from construction to a chemical spill that might prove toxic. They instructed anyone within the zone to remain indoors for their safety, to which civilians immediately agreed upon seeing the firepower brought to bear to secure the roads.

Their efficiency brought satisfaction to Hollis when he arrived. After gaining entry into the zone, the two teams diverged. One gathered before the building in question; the other encircled the far end of the block to wait for instructions. A silent glance passed between Hollis and his second. With merely a nod of acceptance, and the graze of her fingers atop his hand as she exited the vehicle, his second-in-command headed to gather her team for their objective.

Hollis wanted to commend her for her constant diligence. The last eight months had been a pleasure because of her work for the organization. Such compliments were not his style. They were the sign of someone looking for a deeper connection, not the man who had been raised with one mission in mind. His future awaited him.

Compliments weren't necessary or sought after by his second. All that mattered was the mission. Her task was straightforward, with a lone priority: detain the DSA. Hollis knew they were already underfoot. They had been at every event of late. Why would this be any different? Bismarck, however, would not hide them for long. The second team would pick up their trail quickly, ending their nuisance once and for all.

Hollis' own task came with less certainty. The building in question remained a mystery. Upon arriving, the structure appeared dilapidated beyond repair. The second his car entered the cordoned off area of downtown, the building transformed. He saw the spire sparkle against the sunlight. The metal gleamed, spiraling around the entire edifice as if it somehow absorbed the solar rays.

It was a true marvel of engineering.

Hollis approached his waiting team, led by a senior officer from General Adams' branch of the organization: William Lance. Hollis had worked with him well over the years.

"What do we have?"

"Sir," Lance said. His body tensed, tight as a steel pole. "Welcome to Bismarck."

"A dream come true," Hollis replied with a smirk. Lance had always been a stickler for protocol, something Hollis appreciated. What he valued more was the man's devotion to the mission. Adams always lacked the talent, which made their shared commitment to the Trust a battle at times. "What have you found?"

Lance led him to the end of the curb. The entire lobby was in full view. People paid no attention to the situation outside, or to the growing crowd of armed men circling the perimeter.

"There appear to be standard security sweeps." Lance pointed to the men stationed at every corner, and at the base and top of the stairs along the left-hand wall. "One main entrance. The emergency exits are hard-wired. The alarms to breach them can't be accessed from outside. We sent a crew below ground to inspect the electrical lines. They've informed me that if we cut the power to the building, every door will lock instantly. Some kind of security feature in the design, which is also a mystery to my men. They've never seen a setup like it before."

Hollis ran his hand along his chin. "So we are left with only one way in."

Lance nodded.

"Threat level?"

"Minimal," the soldier said. "I count no more than six security guards in the lobby, possibly two more on the second floor landing. However..."

"Yes?"

Lance put his hand on his hip. "I don't know, sir. There's something about the civilians onsite."

Hollis agreed. Their lack of concern was the first tell, but more soon presented. The hairs stood up on the back of Hollis' neck—a sense of something more going on inside the building. He watched the bystanders of the lobby go about their business. Some appeared to be nothing more than tourists, waiting for direction, while most were clearly employees rushing back and forth throughout the floor.

"Tell me what you've noticed," Hollis said. He stared at the lobby intently.

"The same faces the entire time." Lance pointed and drew Hollis' attention. "Some are stationary, sure, like the receptionists and the guards. Others, though, appear to be heading for the stairs and elevators, only to reappear later at the other end of the lobby for another loop. You can almost time the transition."

Hollis understood at once. "Your original assessment was flawed."

"Sir?"

"There are *no* civilians," Hollis said. "*Only* security."

Lance looked at the lobby once more. Recognition filled his brown eyes, and his head lowered. "You're right, sir. I apologize."

"It doesn't matter," Hollis said. "We have the numbers, and the firepower, on our side."

Hollis waved the others in the squad closer. The time for directing traffic was at an end, and they left a single soldier for the menial task to keep pedestrians out of their crosshairs. The soldiers gathered around Hollis. One passed along a weapon for their leader before falling in line with the rest.

Hollis scanned each of their faces. They were the best the military offered, each hand-picked by the Trust because of their skill. Once he held each of them at attention, Hollis pointed to their destination with a smile on his face. "I want what's in that building, soldiers."

They might have been unclear on their task upon arrival, but that was no longer the case. The secrets of the mysterious structure were his for the taking, including those of Zac Modine, who was within and waiting.

"Sir!" a voice shouted from across the street. He held tight to a radio and pushed through the wall of soldiers. "Just received word from Satcom. We have incoming."

"Explain," Hollis ordered.

"A chopper with no media markings," the soldier continued. "No markings of any kind, in fact. It claims to be a sightseeing tour, but refuses to turn around even after being ordered out of the area. It appears to be heading for the structure."

"Clever," Hollis commented. "Shoot it down."

"Sir? Are you sure it's a threat? There's no way to tell from here."

"It's the DSA," Hollis snapped. He snatched the radio from the soldier's hand and loomed over the man. "And never question me again."

The soldier backed away, a nod of apology offered before he melted into the crowd of military personnel. Hollis sighed, then lifted the radio before him.

"This is Hollis," he announced through the line. "We are about to breach the building. I want to make one thing clear: that helicopter is not to reach the roof. Do you understand me? I want it blown out of the sky, and I want it done now."

Hollis didn't wait for confirmation. His orders were not to be taken lightly. He tossed the radio to the cowering simpleton in the crowd, then turned for the building. A glance at the men at his side started their march toward the doors.

"Weapons hot, squad," Hollis said. "Today, we claim the future."

CHAPTER SIXTEEN

The Signal Chamber sat as the crux of the entire building. Halfway up the gleaming spire, the room took up the center of four floors. Computers covered the perimeter, intricate machinery running from the processors on the first level all the way up a series of metal stairs to a terminal at the operation's heart.

The entire apparatus was a wonder to Zac, who stood at the entrance with his mouth agape. Controls were staggered throughout the room. Not an inch of space was wasted. From master panels to auxiliary levers, from diagnostic screens to radio transceivers at the peak of the machine, everything caught Zac's attention.

The central station was built like a box, positioned at the heart of the operation. An energy field made up the walls instead of a physical barrier. Shimmering lights swirled about the chair inside. Atop the seating position were dials and a helmet which connected the entire machine to the transceivers at the peak and the primary controls on the ground level.

"This... This is it," Zac whispered. Raw power surged through the entire room. The sensation sent chills up his arms and down his back. A pulsing wave pulled him deeper into the room. Here, the signal met reality. The chair acted like an interface between the Wellspring and whatever information was pulled from the radio waves. The future was written within these four walls. Zac had reached the end of his journey.

The Emissary prodded him forward. Not that he needed the help. The energy seemed to respond to his presence. The light glow of the box at the center called to him.

"The broadcast hidden behind the carrier waves across the

planet is pulled in and stored in this chamber," she explained without emotion. Every word sounded like a simple statement of fact to her, yet defied all logic in Zac. That amount of information, the idea that it carried the innovations of an entire species, was beyond imagination. The Emissary treated the signal as old hat, rather than a marvel to behold. "We keep the knowledge safe. We maintain the flow. All for it to be absorbed by the Wellspring."

"And then?" Zac uttered. He realized the truth of his position and took a loud gulp of air. "Then I take the knowledge out into the world. I carry out my protocol."

"Yes," the Emissary replied. "Once you complete the initial process."

"Initial process?" The question was lost, however, as the Emissary's heels carried her to the controls on the right side of the ground level.

"Shall we begin?" she asked, a false smile on her face. "I'm sure you're as excited to witness the grand plan the First has provided for us."

Zac's eyes sparked at the mention of the First. The Emissary spoke of the being with an almost pseudo-religious devotion, yet had never mentioned a single fact about the being, including the specifics behind their designation. First of what, exactly?

The question repeated until Zac noticed the woman at the controls was staring at him. She desired a response to start the Wellspring Protocol. Zac gave her a thumbs up.

"Let's do it," he said. "I'm super pumped."

The sarcasm was lost on the woman. She turned away to work on the controls. "I will prepare the chamber. Head to the platform, and we will begin shortly."

"Sounds great." He moved toward her for a better view of the controls. The Emissary shifted closer to the monitors to obstruct his view. When he continued to press for a better vantage, she turned completely from her task.

"The steps will take you to the chamber." Her false smile cracked. Irritation flared for a second, then vanished as if swallowed up.

"Sure." Zac started for the stairs. Heavy footfalls clanged loudly against the metal steps. His hand ran along the railing for support. To his right, the machinery glistened from the light pouring through a row of windows on the uppermost level. The solar rays washed over a series of mirrored circuits and cast their reflection throughout the entire space.

Zac took his time with the ascent. He paused at the landing on the second level for a brief glimpse around the area. Looking over the railing, he threw a smile at the woman below. She tried to reciprocate with a thumbs up of her own, the act awkward and disingenuous like the rest of her.

Zac stepped away from the railing and backed up to the machinery. He caught his reflection along the casing. "Feel like sharing how I stop this thing?"

His tired eyes melted behind those of another. His sunken cheeks and sweaty brow were replaced by April's wrinkled demeanor.

"The chamber is being prepared," she said. Her voice rang louder in his head. It boomed through his mind. Her very presence took over; the persona of the Wellspring quietly replaced his own.

"I'm aware," Zac grumbled under his breath. He slowly climbed to the next level. "But I'm not the Wellspring. Not yet."

"You will be."

Zac gripped the railing tighter. "You told me if I stop this thing, I—"

"I'm well aware of what has been said, Zac," April said. "We're not at the end yet."

"Not according to this Emissary person."

April's eyes thinned. "She's merely a functionary. Not a threat."

"A functionary?" Zac asked. "Like me?"

"Yes."

"And the First? Is it just another protocol or program like the rest?"

April looked away.

Zac stopped at the third landing. He leaned closer to his reflection. "What is it? What is the First?"

"I can't tell you," April replied with sadness behind her words.

"How convenient," Zac muttered.

"The chamber is almost ready," the Emissary called from below. "Please take your position."

Zac continued his climb. "Tell me about the First."

"No."

"I deserve to know," Zac snapped in a muted tone. "This is my life, dammit."

"That life will end when you are given the knowledge," April said. "I've warned you in the past about pushing things too far. About what your curiosity will cost you."

"Yeah, you've warned me, sure," Zac said. "When it's suited your needs. Just like all the information you've graciously passed along. If this First is as much of a threat as it seems, then knowing what it is might help—"

"Enough, Zac," April interrupted. "Nothing will help when it comes to the First. Nothing can stop him once he awakens."

Sadness filled her words. The knowledge held back from him clearly pained her, but she kept it locked away to spare him that same hopelessness.

"He... He's the reason you're helping me."

"I have served his purpose for millennia," April said. "I have offered the world a path that can only lead to him in the end. As much as I've tried to take back what I've wrought, as much as I've hoped to make a difference, this story can only end one way."

"That's not..." Zac slammed his hand against the railing. "You said this ends when the signal is destroyed. You told me I can put a stop to the Wellspring, to whatever path we're on, by coming here. Was that all a lie?"

April wasn't looking at him any longer. She turned away toward the steps. "She's coming."

"No," Zac bristled. "You need to talk to me. You need to tell me what I'm supposed to do. What's the right choice?"

"You'll know the right choice when the time comes, Zac." April faded from view. Zac closed his eyes to focus on her image, but she slipped away. Her last words were little more than a whisper. "You have to hurry."

The Emissary stood at the second landing. "It is time, Zachary."

Zac nodded. At the fourth, and final, level, he moved for the glowing box in the center of the room. Electricity charged through him even from a distance, yet he pressed forward.

"Step through and see the possibilities unlock in your mind."

It was the first time he heard anticipation in the Emissary's voice—excitement at what came next. It scared the crap out of Zac.

His hand touched the energy field surrounding the chamber. His mind screamed at the interaction. He thought he was screaming as well. Pulling back, Zac realized the truth: the gleam of daylight in the room became replaced with crimson. The windows shut and locked. All around him, alarms blared.

Something had gone horribly wrong.

CHAPTER SEVENTEEN

Nixon passed the time as only he could: by going through the belongings of his teammates. He treated the snooping as a cataloging exercise. It rationalized the necessity in his eyes and made him feel useful despite being left behind.

Morgan's decision still rankled Nixon. There was no reason to bench him from the field. He had done well on the missions he had been present for during his brief stay with the DSA. There had been no complaints about his performance, at least none made directly to him at any rate.

Maybe it was Adler? Had he gone too far with her, been a little too cordial? Societal norms were not Nixon's strengths. While he might have thought the banter between them appropriate, the opposite might have also been true. He never was one for playing by the rules. He viewed that as an admirable skill, not a detriment to his ability to perform his job.

The snooping went a bit overboard, though. It started innocently enough with a peek in Metcalf's abandoned quarters. Her departure had rattled Nixon—especially after bringing him onto the team so recently. He simply hadn't had the time to get to know the others as much. Metcalf's living space had been sparse; Kanigher must have cleaned after she'd left. After pawing through a few drawers, Nixon had moved on to more exciting terrain.

Ben's quarters were a wonderland. The man owned more toys than a child. His so-called reading material comprised a pile of vintage comic books stacked in the corner of his bed, and the instruction manual to an unopened smoothie machine.

Nixon headed for Adler's room next. He wanted to save her

for last, but his curiosity got the better of him. Her room was pristine. The desk had been cleaned off, and the bed had been made. Even in her rush to leave, Adler had tucked everything away—from clothes to the few belongings she'd brought with her. There were books, of course. Her interests varied throughout the genres. Science and technology sat next to urban fantasy, which leaned against historical romance.

He hadn't joined the team for something as mundane as love. What had brought him to the fold had been the Trust. Their controlling interest in the world was a true menace, and for so long, he had been the only one to see it. The DSA changed that for him.

Adler, though, changed more for him. Her smile opened doors in his mind, and in his heart. Nixon stopped short of her closet doors. Snooping might have been one of his favorite pastimes, but it probably wouldn't do him any favors with the others. He left the room before pressing his luck any further.

He stopped short of Simon Holbrook's room. Their newest addition brought with him a feeling of unease in Nixon. He couldn't say why. It might have been the way Morgan had gone around the rest of them to invite the man to the Bunker in the first place. Or was it in the way Holbrook looked at them during their introduction, as if he were inspecting new patients? Something unsettled Nixon when he thought about the man. He reached for the knob, then let the suspicion and his curiosity fall away. There would be plenty of time later. Work awaited him.

Operations sat cold and desolate in the absence of everyone else. Nixon threw on a sweatshirt upon entering and tucked his hands in the pockets. All the systems ran on automatic; the surveillance on the building in question linked with Adler's tablet. She never let the device leave her side, so any monitoring on his end would only amount to more snooping.

Everything ran through the hub, yet all was superfluous to the team's needs. Nixon tracked phone traffic in the area, call signs, specific search patterns, and more through the system. Nothing appeared out of sorts.

It wasn't until he stepped into Operations that Nixon realized how wrong he truly was. Chatter rang out through the comm lines. Air Traffic asked questions, then received orders to ignore from a third party.

Nixon sat down. He pulled on his headset and dove into the system. All the chatter related to a chopper in the area: Ben and Morgan's chopper.

"Oh hell," he muttered. Nixon threw the set off his ears to grab for the internal comm. Slipping the earpiece into place, Nixon tapped the call button three times. "Come on, Alison, pick up. Pick up the damn—"

"Nixon?" Adler said through the line. "Why are you yelling?"

"Alison! Oh, thank God. Listen—"

"You're screaming, Nixon," Adler said. "Take a breath."

"No time."

"Make the time," she replied. "For the sake of my ears."

Nixon shut his mouth. He forced a cleansing breath through his nose.

"Feeling better?"

"Not a bit," he said. "Now listen—"

"I was going to call you soon, actually."

"Really?"

"I wanted to make sure you weren't going through our closets or anything." She chuckled at the idea, and his cheeks burned red. "You haven't, have you?"

"No," he answered, drawing out the word. "Well, yes. But not yours. I would never—"

"Nixon..."

"It doesn't matter," Nixon said. "Listen to me. They know."

"What?" Adler asked, confused. "Who knows what?"

"I just picked up local chatter about a strange chopper." Nixon returned to the terminal. His eyes widened at the latest to come across the wire. "Someone has issued orders to take it down."

"Take it down?"

"The helicopter!" Nixon shouted. "The Trust knows you're coming, Alison. Get the team the hell out of there, and do it now!"

CHAPTER EIGHTEEN

"We're coming up on the target," Davey shouted through the internal headset. Morgan shifted from her seat for a better look. Her tension continued to rise, her fists clenched tight before her. Every attempt to loosen her up, to relax her, had failed on Ben's part. He simply hoped she would find her rhythm once they reached the spire.

"I see it." Morgan pointed ahead. Ben joined her, glancing out the windshield at their approaching destination. The gleaming building was obvious against the rest of the skyline. Morgan's brow furrowed. "How can I see it?"

"What do you mean?" Ben asked.

"You told me it was cloaked, or hidden from view," she replied. "That when you looked at the place, there was nothing but a wreck of a building."

"She's right," Davey chimed in. "I've passed overhead a couple hundred times over the years, and I've never seen that rooftop before."

"So what changed?"

Ben shrugged. "Maybe it has something to do with us stepping through the illusion earlier?"

"If that's the case, the place is completely exposed to everyone, isn't it? That means—"

"The Trust," Ben said with a wince. "Nothing like a little more pressure to set the tone for us."

"It gets worse," Davey remarked. "I can't land on that small of a strip. Best I can do is get close for you to jump."

"Jump?" Morgan exclaimed. She shook her head. "I'd rather take my chances with the front entrance."

"No, you wouldn't," Ben said, recalling the crowd below. "It won't be far, Morgan. Right, Davey?"

"Nothing more than a big first step," the pilot answered with a grin. "Scout's honor."

"See?" Ben commented, a hand on Morgan's shoulder. "Davey was a scout. How can you not trust a scout?"

"I hate you."

"Love," Ben corrected. "You meant to say love."

"Get ready," Davey said. He pitched the copter lower. With the turn, both Ben and Morgan clutched tight to their seats. "Here we—"

A glint of light shone in the distance. It reflected the sun toward them. From behind the light came a blast of smoke that streaked into the sky.

"Shit," Davey said.

Ben followed the man's gaze. "What is that?"

Morgan's hands dug into the fabric of her chair. "It's coming right for us."

Davey turned toward them. "You have to go. Now."

"What?" Morgan cried. "We're too high. We need to—"

"Don't argue with me," Davey yelled. "Go!"

The glint faded from the object before them. Ben glimpsed the metal casing behind the shine. The projectile's trajectory was clear, the target all too obvious.

"We're going." Ben unbuckled, stood, then opened the door. Morgan had been right. They were positioned over the rooftop, but the height was problematic, to say the least. The lack of parachutes, or any sort of prep time, added to the growing list of concerns. "Morgan?"

"Ben, there is no way—"

He uncoupled her belt. Pulling her to her feet, Ben dragged her for the open door. Wind whipped her hair over her face, yet through her black curls, frightened eyes stared at him.

"Jump!" Davey screamed. "God dammit, jump!"

Ben took a deep breath.

"Ben?" Morgan said, her voice barely a whisper through the wind.

"Sorry, Morgan. This is gonna hurt."

"Don't you—"

He grabbed her and leaped out the side of the copter. Tucking Morgan close, Ben forced her head to his chest and wrapped his arms around her like a blanket. The best it accomplished was to muffle Morgan's scream.

A view of the rooftop came in fast below. Ben led with his feet. There had been no time for thought, no time to worry about how the wind might take them off target.

Both crashed hard against the roof. Their bodies crumpled upon impact, bending at the knees before rolling forward. Their momentum carried them across the gravel-coated surface. Stones dug into exposed skin, and Ben forced his eyes shut to avoid a stray rock.

Their bodies, still locked together, bounded for the far edge. They slammed into the pipes jutting out from the center of the roof. Ben let go of Morgan with one hand and grabbed for the obstruction to halt their momentum. Morgan slipped away from him. Her fingers caught hold of another pipe to the left. The ventilation pipe dug into Ben's skin, the metal sharp as a knife's blade, but he held on until the world righted itself and his body stopped shaking.

Ben struggled to catch his breath. Blood trickled from his fingers. Standing, Ben helped Morgan to her feet. "You okay?"

She pushed the hair away from her face. A cut ran across her forehead. Blood streaked through her hair like a highlight. Nothing appeared broken, though. They had made it, but concern still won out.

Morgan pointed to the sky. "The pilot. Davey, he—"

The missile crashed through the front of the copter. The force of the explosion shattered the cabin and engulfed the entire helicopter in a fireball. Davey was gone, all trace of the man lost in an instant.

The copter hung in the sky for a brief second. The propeller ground to a halt. Fire continued to rage throughout the cabin, which set off smaller explosions from the fuel tanks. Then, the wreckage began to fall toward the rooftop.

"Ben—"

He grabbed her hand. "Move, Morgan. Move!"

They dove away from the ventilation pipe for the door to the building below. The heat from the burning copter seared their backs as they crashed into the gravel. Their bodies slid into the shadows of the door, and they tucked close to the wall for support.

The copter slammed into the rooftop. Propeller blades cut into the stone. Rock and debris kicked up from the crash and showered them as the wreckage continued to slide closer to the edge. Grinding metal pummeled the rooftop; the blades bent and sheared off the still burning cabin. For a moment, the helicopter lurched over the edge, threatening the street below. With a slight heave, almost like breathing, the cabin fell back to the stone of the roof with a deafening thud.

Morgan's hand ripped away from Ben. She rushed to the cabin. "Davey!"

Before she could reach the burning metal, Ben pulled her back and held her close. "He's gone, Morgan."

She stared at the flames with tears in her eyes. "There's nothing we can do," Ben said. "We have to go on. We have to find Zac."

Morgan's knees gave way, and she collapsed on the roof. "I can't do this anymore, Ben. I just can't do this anymore."

CHAPTER NINETEEN

"What do I do?" Zac whispered. He glanced around at the flashing red lights. The alarms continued to blare. They drowned out his frantic mutterings. "Tell me what I'm supposed to do."

Behind him, the Emissary's heels clacked against the metal steps. She was getting closer. Whatever Zac had done when he touched the energy field must have set off the alarm. If she stopped him from entering the chamber, then all his efforts had been for nothing.

"Help me," Zac pleaded.

April's visage shimmered along the energy field. "This isn't you, Zac. This is something else."

The news failed to slow his heart. "It doesn't matter. She's coming for me, and I don't even know how to breach the chamber, or what I'm supposed to do inside."

"Take a breath, Zac," April said. "Once you connect with the field, it will read you. You'll be granted entry into the chamber. There are a series of mental switches to activate after the transmission synchronizes with your thought patterns."

"But you said only the Wellspring can enter the chamber," Zac said. "The Emissary said the same thing. If I pass through the field—"

"Zac." April stopped his spiraling thoughts. "Disrupting the signal is the only way this ends."

"As the Wellspring," Zac said. "This is why you sent me, why you've pushed me to this point. So you can take over."

"I am trying to help you. That's all I've ever done."

"That's a lie."

"That's the truth," she shot back. "The only truth you need to hear right now. Zac, for too long I have guided humanity toward an inescapable future, one that will come when this signal reaches terminal point. That day is soon, far sooner than anyone believes, but if you help me — if you allow me to help you — we can stop it today."

"I..." Zac held up his hand to the field. A wave of energy ran up his arm at the merest touch. "I don't know if I can—"

"Stop!"

Zac turned back to see the Emissary at the landing. She held out her hand and her steps quickened at his shift toward the chamber.

"Ignore her," April called. Zac spun back to the energy field. "You can feel the change coursing through you. Let it in. Let *me* in fully."

Zac pushed his hands through the field. His foot crashed into the cascading energy surrounding the chamber. He closed his eyes and leaned his head toward the blinding light.

A hand closed around his arm. Extreme force yanked him clear of the field. Zac slammed into the railing, and nearly toppled over the ledge. His eyes widened in a panic. The Emissary maintained a firm grip to keep him at her side.

"Did you not hear me?"

"Th—the signal," Zac stammered. He pointed to the chamber, just out of reach, yet so far away now. "I was—"

"Come with me," the Emissary ordered. She set him on his feet and prodded him down the steps. Zac tried to pull away. The chamber was his only escape, but her hand remained locked around his arm.

"What about the signal?"

"It can wait." Her hurried steps caused him to trip on their descent. She held him at her side, squeezing tight with each stumble.

"What's happened?" Zac asked. *What did I do wrong?*

"The building has been breached. Your safety supersedes all other directives."

"My safety? I'm fine. You can let me go."

"Not yet." They reached the lowest level in the room. The alarms continued out in the corridor. They left the four-story space to circle the perimeter of the building. A few women stood near the elevator. They tracked any incoming traffic with blank stares. The Emissary let Zac go for a brief second to collect the small group. "You will remain on this floor. I will send for more hands as soon as I am apprised of the situation in full."

The women offered no responses. Eyes blinked rapidly, as if absorbing their instructions, then the group returned their attention to the exit points on the floor. Along each of their necks, barely visible from their collared shirts, Zac noticed a white patch. A blue glow emanated from the center.

The Emissary turned back to Zac. "They will keep you secure."

"I'm already secure," he replied. "I feel very secure. Honest."

She snatched his arm once more. Dragging him around the corner, she opened the first door on the right and shoved Zac forward into the room. It was vacant, devoid of all furniture. The only thing present was the whistling of air through the rectangular vent cover on the back wall.

"You will stay here until it is safe," the Emissary said.

"What are you going to do?"

The Emissary eyed him curiously. "Directives state no one may enter the facility without authorization. Fail-safe Protocol will be initiated to deal with the intruders."

"Fail-safe Protocol?" Zac asked. "What is Fail-safe Protocol?"

"Let it go, Zac," April warned within his mind.

The Emissary ignored the question. Her hand fell on the door and began to close it in his face.

"Wait!"

"You will remain here for the duration," the Emissary instructed. "This room is secure from the threat."

"What threat?" Zac said. "What intruders?"

"Do not concern yourself," the woman answered. "Fail-safe Protocol will be initiated momentarily. They will be dealt with. Swiftly and permanently."

The door slammed shut. Zac grabbed at the handle. It refused to turn, locked from the outside. He pounded at the metal slab.

"Hey! You can't just leave me here!"

No answer came. The clacking of heels faded in the distance. Zac fell away from the door. The signal had been within his grasp, and he'd let it slip through his fingers. As long as the signal remained active, his life was in jeopardy. Now, however, he could do nothing but wait. Zac worried he had lost his one chance at freedom and wondered what else would go wrong before the day was out.

CHAPTER TWENTY

With the M16 tight in his grasp, and his pistol hugging his left hip, Hollis entered the mysterious spire. Lance and the rest of his team of fifteen soldiers followed close behind.

"Take up positions," Hollis said as soon as he cracked the door open. "Hold fire until I give the order."

"Yes, sir." Lance motioned for the team to split. Hollis took a single step past the doors, and in that moment his squad separated and spread along the front wall of the building. All were armed with the same weaponry. Body armor protected their torsos.

No one flinched at their presence. Not a single soul looked in their direction, despite the stomping of boots on the ground. The movements monitored prior to their entry continued. The pattern of motion with each employee remained unchanged. Muttering from the receptionists at the desk to the right never skipped a beat. Children in the tour group listened in for their instructions. Nothing deterred the people in the lobby from their tasks.

"What the hell?" Lance muttered. "What is wrong with these people?"

Hollis held up a hand. The commentary wasn't required. Besides, *people* might have been the wrong word to use for those in the lobby. People varied, they adapted to outside stimuli. These beings, trapped in their circular pattern—forever looped on repeat—took no notice of anything other than the role they played in keeping up the structure's appearances.

Approaching the reception desk, the woman at the end of the row greeted Hollis. She lowered the microphone to her headset, ignoring the monotonous ringing of her extension, to smile at the newcomer. The curling of her lips caused her head to twitch, like the effort was counter to her innate programming.

"Can I help you with something, sir?"

"Yes," Hollis replied. He lowered his weapon on the counter above her. "Dreadful things always get in the way, don't they?"

"Can I help you with something, sir?"

Hollis huffed at the repeated question. "You're going to be insufferably useless, aren't you?" He picked up the gun and took aim. "Perhaps this won't be as in the way as I had thought. Now tell me what this place is, and what you do here."

The receptionist stared down the barrel of the weapon. Her smile remained in place, her cold eyes a void of emotion. "Can I... help..."

Her body collapsed over her station. Her face slammed into the keyboard, and the headset fell off and clattered along the desk. One by one, each of the receptionists followed suit, like their bodies simply quit on them.

"Sir?" Lance called from his position at the door.

Every person in the room stopped moving. Their patterns disrupted, each individual—from employee to security to visitor—slumped over where they stood. They remained on their feet, those standing at any rate, while the rest crashed over chairs and to the floor.

A hand fell on Hollis' shoulder. It caused him to jump slightly. Lance stood at his side, though he backed off at the sight of Hollis' reaction.

"Sorry, sir," Lance said.

Hollis grimaced. "You damn well better be."

"What do we do about this?" Lance asked. "How should we proceed?"

"We hold for the moment." Hollis crept up to the closest employee. They had been in mid-stride on a loop toward the elevators at the rear of the lobby. The excitement in their faces had been wiped clean, much like their purpose. Hollis reached to check their pulse when the figure stirred.

"Get back, sir." Lance raised his weapon.

"Stand down," Hollis snapped. The being in mid-stride shuffled to stand upright. Everyone in the room stood at attention from their once-collapsed position. They turned away from their previous tasks and conversations, their full focus on the soldiers along the front wall.

Where once they noticed jubilant looks on the faces of the men and women in the mysterious structure, now Hollis and his team faced blank expressions with eyes faded to white.

"Fail-safe Protocol initiated," the receptionist chanted from her station.

"Fail-safe Protocol initiated," the others in the room repeated. They all spoke in the same monotonous tone, all personalities wiped from them as easily as their eyes had been.

"Sir?" Lance called from behind Hollis. Fear filled the man's voice, just as it crept through Hollis' entire body. His desire for answers led him to this moment. He refused to let his chance at understanding slip away.

He held firm and brought his weapon to bear. "They aren't human. Not anymore."

The crowd responded in kind at his aggressive stance and took a step toward the intruders in their midst. "Fail-safe Protocol initiated. Subdue all intruders for the integration process. All serve the First and the glory to come."

"The First?" Hollis asked.

Lance's hands shook against his weapon. "Sir?"

Hollis nodded to him, then disengaged the safety on his M16. He peered down the row to each of his squad, then the other side. "I want what is hiding in this building. Kill them all."

Screams accompanied them as his team opened fire on the civilians rushing toward their position. The fight had begun.

CHAPTER TWENTY-ONE

The flames from the wreckage nipped at her skin. Morgan sat before the burned-out cabin and stared deep into the well of colors that soared into the air. They shifted to deep black as they rose above the skyline and out among the clouds.

"He's dead," Morgan whispered. Their pilot was ash, dead the moment the rocket slammed into their copter. "He didn't even have a damn chance."

"No," Ben said. His hand curled under her arms. "But he gave us one."

Ben tried to pull her back to her feet. She resisted, unable to leave the gravel-coated ground that dominated the rooftop. She didn't want to move, couldn't stop looking at the burning wreck before her. A man was dead, and there was no Metcalf to blame this time. Morgan was the one in charge. Her inability to foresee the threat made it no less damning.

Unable to drag her away from the copter, Ben circled around. Once in front of her, he crouched to block her view. "Morgan, we need to move. The Trust is obviously onsite, so our timetable went from minutes to seconds to find Zac."

Morgan tilted her head over Ben's shoulder. Through the flames, she thought she glimpsed Davey still smoldering in his seat. "I was in charge, Ben. I took charge of the team, and someone is already dead."

His hands reached out. Clasping the sides of her head, Ben forced Morgan to look at him and only him. "You are not to blame, Morgan. That? What happened to Davey? That's not on you. That's on the Trust. Remember that and pay them back in kind."

When his hands fell away, Ben stood. He paced the length of the roof. His sidearm was in his hands. The weapon led his scan of the area for additional threats. Morgan never thought to check, never looked past the damage that had been done.

What kind of leader sits and wallows in their mistakes? she thought. *Not the kind I want to be, that's for damn sure.*

Her limbs ached from their fall, her knees scraped up. Blood caked to her forehead along a thin gash. It pulsed with pain, but Morgan swallowed it down as she stood. "Ben?"

"Yeah?"

"Thank you."

At her words, the door to the roof slammed open. Men in deep blue shirts carrying Glocks stormed the area and spread in front of the door. Eight men blocked their escape from the roof. They took aim at the two intruders.

Ben dropped his gun to his feet, then raised his hands. "Maybe don't thank me yet."

"Down on the ground!" one of the security guards shouted. Half the squad focused on Ben. The other turned toward Morgan, fury in their eyes.

Morgan lowered to her knees. "Listen to me. I know how this looks, but we're federal agents attempting to secure a vital witness to—"

All eight men dropped their weapons to the ground. In an instant, they bent at their waists, arms outstretched toward their feet. They offered no sound, no explanation for the sudden shift.

Ben nearly cheered. He leaped into the air and clapped his hands with excitement. "Holy crap! Did you just bullshit them to death, Morgan? Is that your new superpower?"

Morgan held back her irritation. Concern filled her. No matter the threat against them, these eight men were innocent. Getting to her feet, she made her way over to the closest one. Morgan lifted his hand and let it go. The appendage fell limply before him once more. She shifted to the next. Bending low for a closer look, she inspected his eyes. They remained opened, but took in no stimuli.

"I don't understand."

"It's called a lucky break," Ben said.

"Does that sound like something that happens to us?" Morgan circled the group. There were no signs of life, like they had simply shut down. "A systemic collapse like that? For all of them? What is going on here?"

"We should get moving." Ben shifted past the fallen men for the door.

"Hold up, Ben," Morgan called after him. He turned to her, confused. "We can't leave them like this."

"We have to find Zac."

"And we will, but not at the cost of innocent lives," Morgan said.

Ben smirked. "I was wondering when you'd start sounding like the Morgan I know and love." His cheeks flushed. "You know what I mean."

"I'm starting to," she said. The pressure of taking over the team had unsettled her. Morgan's balance had been off; the new job took precedence over her own instincts. Seeing the men before her snapped something loose inside, and it felt damn good. It felt right. "Now help me figure out how to save these guys."

Ben nodded. He headed toward her, then stopped. One man stirred, fingers curling before him. "Did you do something?"

"Not yet," Morgan replied. They backed away from the group. The eight men before them stood upright in unison. Their furious eyes were replaced with blank white orbs which stared through the two intruders. "What happened?"

"You know..." Ben shifted closer to her. He picked up his weapon and clutched it tight to his side. "I'm fine not knowing the answer to that question."

"Fail-safe Protocol initiated," all eight men said together. It echoed over the crackling flames of the copter. Their voices were an almost robotic monotone.

"See?" Ben muttered. "That's the kind of stuff I don't want to hear."

The security forces took a step forward. They spoke as one. "Subdue intruders for integration."

"That sounds less than pleasant," Ben said. He lifted his pistol at them. Taking a step in front of Morgan, he tried to shield her from what came next.

Instead, Morgan knocked his arm down. "What are you doing? You can't shoot them. They're still people."

"They sure as hell aren't acting like people!"

Ben was right in that regard. Their movements, as well as

their very speech pattern, were completely in sync with those around them. Individuality had left the security force, now replaced with a single aim. They didn't even bother with their fallen weapons. They merely reached out, ready to ensnare the trapped agents.

"Doesn't matter," Morgan said. She had no idea if they were people or not. She refused to add to the body count. Killing them wouldn't save them from whatever program had taken them over. "We can't risk a firefight with them right now."

"Then how do we get to the door, Morgan?" Ben continued to shield her from the approaching men. His shuffling steps pushed her closer and closer to the edge of the roof. Their options quickly ran out.

"We don't."

Morgan turned to the ventilation duct at their back. Pulling out her Glock, Morgan opened fire at the grate covering the pipe. Twin bullets punctured the set screws, and the grating slipped free. It clattered against the stone.

"Move it, Ben."

Ben peered back at the vent. He shook his head. "Really, Morgan? I have a bad feeling—"

"Don't care," she snapped. The men were almost on top of them. Morgan yanked Ben by his collar. "Move!"

Ben dove into the open vent. Morgan clambered into the duct, then paused. She eyed the eight men once more, saddened at their unknown affliction. She wanted answers—more than anything, she wanted to save them. However, she also worried any action on her part would add eight more casualties on the day. Morgan slipped into the vent, letting the darkness envelop her.

CHAPTER TWENTY-TWO

The safe house wasn't ideal. There were too many entry points to cover. The sheer size alone made it unwieldy. The alley to the rear was narrow, but wide enough for transport. If blocked by the road, there would only be one way out from the entire building—through an overhead door that led to what must have been a loading zone at some point.

Kanigher tried not to complain about the setup. Their prep time had been limited. The flight over had offered a narrow window for research and selection. Morgan, however, had foregone advice on the subject. He understood her position—the new leader tried to make a good first impression on the team. It came at the expense of his knowledge of the area, and her dismissal of his advice felt more like punishment than leadership.

Relegated to the role of soldier and little else, Kanigher did what he had always done: he worked the job. Even after his assignment to stay at the safe house for what amounted to babysitting duty, Kanigher buttoned his lips and set about the task.

Finishing another circuit around the facility, Kanigher left the confines of the alley. The interior was open for the most part. The garage that led to the alley gave clear access to a meeting area where the rest of the team was stationed. That room fed into a small hallway with a bathroom and kitchen. Heading in the opposite direction took them upstairs to a series of offices and converted bedrooms.

Kanigher stuck with the first floor. He looped around the garage, where the van faced the exit with the keys in the ignition, then continued into the meeting room, which overlooked the street outside. Adler and Holbrook sat around a small wooden table. It wasn't level and tilted with each movement. Adler grumbled about the conditions while working on her tablet. Holbrook tapped along his legs to the beat of her keystrokes. Every few seconds, he shifted his weight. The table followed suit, which caused more grumbles from Adler.

"Any word?" Kanigher asked upon entering. He took up his station near the window. The street outside was quiet, the late afternoon traffic not yet hitting the area. Few pedestrians wandered about the sidewalk. They were off the beaten path, with no real hotspots available on the block.

Adler shook her head at the question. "I can't raise anyone on the copter. I lost the feed from their body cams. No video or audio. Everything's de—"

"Nixon tell us anything?"

"Sat link picked up an explosion," Adler replied. "It's taken out his view."

Kanigher's jaw tightened. Being cut out of the action grated on his every nerve. He wanted to scream.

Holbrook stood up from the table. The sudden movement caused the rickety furniture to wobble. Adler held tight to the leg for support. She waited for it to settle before continuing to look into the situation at the spire. Holbrook paced the room. The floor creaked under his every step.

On his third lap, Adler lowered her tablet. "Didn't bring anything to do?"

Holbrook shrugged. "Only packed medical supplies. It's my first 'mission.' I can't believe you guys actually call it that."

"Morgan likes to tell people they'll get used to it," Adler said with a comforting smile. It was a gift she shared with everyone around her. Her charm failed to penetrate Holbrook's reticence, though.

"I don't think that's going to happen," he said.

Adler grabbed her bag near her feet. Sifting through the contents inside, she pulled out a book. "Here. I'm finished with it."

Holbrook held up his hand. "I've already read it."

Adler extended the book. "It will take your mind off things."

Holbrook shook his head. "I'm good. They might need me. I should be ready for, well, anything, right?"

Kanigher shot the man a thin glare. "Take the book."

The timid doctor glimpsed Kanigher's sidearm. His pacing

slowed until he made it back to the table. He reached for the book. "Well, I guess I could use a little distraction."

"And I could use a little less of one," Adler commented. Holbrook sat back down to thumb through the text. Each page turn sounded like a passing car in the quiet of the room. Adler slowly lowered the tablet. Curiosity filled her face.

"You're staring at me. Am I still making too much noise?"

"You are, but it's not that." Adler leaned closer. "You've had plastic surgery."

"I—" The observation clearly flustered him. He closed the book, a hand to his face to shield it from view.

Kanigher turned from the window. He had only known the doctor for a few hours, but everything about Holbrook rubbed Kanigher the wrong way. He wasn't built for field work, and his qualifications as a physician were dubious considering the circumstances of their introduction. Personality traits had been the extent of what Kanigher had learned about the new member, given their limited time together. Still, the moment Adler mentioned his physical alterations, Kanigher couldn't help but notice the same thing.

"Don't get me wrong, it's very subtle work," Adler continued. Holbrook lowered his hand and gave her a full view of his face. "Your cheekbones. Your nose. Your chin. Anywhere else?"

Holbrook smiled. "You show me yours, and I'll show you mine."

Adler laughed. "Right. Sorry. I tend to overstep when it comes to analyzing."

Kanigher disagreed with her assessment. Every observation was critical to understanding a situation. To Kanigher, Holbrook stood as a complete unknown. Any insight into the man offered a better picture of his capabilities—and his secrets.

Holbrook opened the book, his wishes made clear by his silence. Reading failed, however, and he closed the text once again. A sigh escaped his lips.

"There was an accident," he said. "I made a mistake, a slip in judgment, you might say. At least I acquired a new me out of the deal."

Adler nodded, then let the issue drop. Kanigher wanted to hear more, but his attention returned to the window and the street outside. Adler set her tablet down on the table to join him.

"Sounds like we've found another broken soldier," Kanigher muttered.

A sad look passed from Adler to the reading doctor. "He should fit right in, then."

"We'll see."

Adler leaned against the frame of the window. "You think they made it out of the chopper in time?"

"They made it," Kanigher said without hesitation. "They did."

He kept his eyes locked on the outside, away from her. Kanigher needed that distance. Any thought of the copter sent the worst-case scenarios spiraling through his mind. If the team was down, what happened next? And if they made it to the rooftop, why hadn't they reached out?

Adler took his distance as a sign of rejection. She pushed from the window, her gaze low to the ground. "I'll let you do your work."

"Adler," he called after her. "Alison. I'm sorry. It's just—"

"I understand," Adler said. "Metcalf leaving has us all reeling. We all need time to figure things out. Find our place on the team, and with each other."

"It's not—" A shift of color from the periphery pulled him back to the window. Kanigher released his weapon from his holster.

"What?" Adler asked. "What is it?"

Kanigher tucked close to the wall. "Movement."

A car parked at the end of the block with blacked-out windows. Kanigher moved to the other side of the window to see another car at the next intersection. Shadows shifted along the ground. Steps closed in from all sides.

"How bad?"

Kanigher pulled Adler away from the windows. "We're blown." He lifted her tablet from the table and tossed it to her. "Pack up everything you can carry. We need to leave. Now."

CHAPTER TWENTY-THREE

The screams came not from their victims, but from Hollis' men themselves. They cried out as they mowed down the blank-eyed men, women, and children in the lobby. The first wave fell in seconds. Dozens of bodies littered the floor.

With each fallen enemy, Hollis and his team advanced deeper into the building. They offered no remorse, no prayers for the dead. The building's fail-safe gave the soldiers an excuse to slaughter any impediment to their goal.

For a solid minute, Hollis believed himself to be indestructible. It was his destiny to find this place, to discover the true future for humanity and the reason behind it. Nothing could stand against him. Nothing would hold him back or push him from his path.

The tide, however, quickly turned against Hollis and his team. They believed the individuals against them were powerless, that their slow, deliberate steps kept them from being a real danger. The truth told a different tale. With each fallen automaton, the rest of the room hastened in their assault. As the dozens died under the onslaught of gunfire, those at the rear of the lobby sped up in their opposition. Longer strides took over from shuffling feet, and their mobility immediately sent Hollis' team back to a defensive posture.

The first of Hollis' men fell near the stairs. They failed to consider the change in the threat's behavior. One guard at the top of the steps leaped down. Ducking under a strike by the soldier, the guard didn't hit back. No physical confrontation on their part took place. The guard merely removed an object from his pocket and slapped it against the soldier's neck.

The white patch lit up in sharp blue, like the contents had been activated. Panic filled the soldier. A cry not of aggression, but pure fear echoed over the roar of the gunfire. A second later, the soldier collapsed. Like the employees and guards before him, the soldier stood bent over in standby mode for a full minute.

When he returned to life, his eyes—once a muddy brown—changed to stark white to match the rest of the protocol-laden brethren in the room. "Fail-safe Protocol initiated."

He was but the first to fall under their sway. With every step deeper into the mysterious structure, Hollis lost another soldier to the opposition. They collapsed with the implantation of the strange patch, only to revive and add to the enemy's numbers. Half of Hollis' team was taken out in the time it took to cross the lobby.

"What do we do now?" Lance asked in a panic.

"What we have to," Hollis replied. He took aim. He knew the names of each of the men, had brought them into the Trust for their diligence and their sense of duty. They were irreplaceable. Unfortunately, they also stood in Hollis' way. He opened fire and cut them down.

"Sir!" Lance cried. "You can't!"

Hollis didn't stop. He didn't hesitate to end the threat against the remaining members of his team. A long, strafing line of fire brought his soldiers down.

He turned to Lance, breathing hard and bloodthirsty as hell. "Nothing stops us from our task. Nothing! Do you understand?"

Lance nodded with terror in his eyes. "Yes, sir."

"Good."

"Where do we go now?" he said. "There are more coming from the upper levels."

"Scatter," Hollis ordered to those left. "Pair up and find a defensible position. I don't care how long it takes, or how many fall today. We don't leave this building until we find what we're looking for."

A pair of soldiers moved for the stairs. Gunfire paved their way up to the second floor. Another pair moved for the corridor along the right. Hollis and Lance headed left.

"Sir? No disrespect meant, but what do you hope to find here? These people—"

"Aren't people," Hollis snapped. "Not anymore, Lance. And

the truth is what we're after today."

"The truth?"

Hollis didn't bother to answer the man's question. For too long, Hollis had followed the path blindly. He had recruited the best and brightest, all at the whim of the Wellspring's direction. Every advancement had come from her, every step forward a degree of success, but for whom in the end? The Trust needed to make the next leap on their own. The future was meant for them to shape, to wield, and ultimately to control.

Distracted by his own thoughts, Hollis barely noticed the newcomers to the corridor until it was too late. They breached the office doors on either side. Their hands reached for Hollis with the same patch that had taken out half his team. The first earned a bullet to the head for the attempt. The second — a woman in a pale blue dress — drew too close. Without a clear shot, Hollis lashed out and slammed the butt of his weapon into the woman's chin. She crashed through the drywall. Hollis pulled back, then hit the trigger to end her shuffling.

"Sir!"

Six more targets flanked them from the rear. They had snuck up on Lance somehow. They pulled at the soldier's arms for some exposed skin. Two carried the device to overtake the man, unable to get close enough as Lance kicked at them for his freedom.

"Help me, sir!"

Hollis pulled Lance loose from the crowd. The terrified soldier was not the man Hollis had believed him to be such a short time ago. The fear was unbecoming of the role they played for the rest of humanity. It sickened Hollis.

Looking past Lance at the rest of the corridor, more than a dozen indoctrinated souls raced for their position. They were about to be overrun.

"Thank you, thank you."

"No, soldier," Hollis said. He ripped the man's weapon from his hands. Lance's eyes widened. "Thank *you*... for your service."

"Sir, wait—"

Hollis shoved Lance toward the pack. He needed the distraction. The mindless souls swallowed Lance's body whole. They ripped at his clothes to expose his flesh to their patch.

Hollis ran from the scene. The seconds ticked by, precious time he required to get some breathing room. Lance's weapon brought with it a sense of relief, and he strapped the spare firearm over his shoulder.

Turning the corner, Hollis found the stairs to the upper floors. He reached for the handle and the door burst open. More blank-eyed souls poured out. They clawed at the air for him to join them.

"Fail-safe Protocol initiated," they said in unison.

Hollis backpedaled for safety. He peered down the first hall, only to see Lance at the head of the pack moving for Hollis' position.

"Fail-safe Protocol initiated," the former soldier said in a dead tone.

"Dammit," Hollis muttered. He turned and fled. The corridor offered no escape. A lone door sat at the end. Hollis opened it and jumped inside. He slipped the lock into place.

Bodies crashed into the panel. The door threatened to collapse in on itself. Hollis glanced around for more support. The room was little more than a closet. Shelving lined the right-hand wall. Hollis tipped the entire structure over. The shelves fell before the door at an angle and barred all entry into the space.

Hollis fell to the floor. He grabbed at his chest to slow his breathing, to calm his shivering body. There was no way in for the enemy and no way out for him. Hollis had no plan, no exit strategy, to survive the hour, let alone the day. All he could do was wait it out and pray for his salvation.

CHAPTER TWENTY-FOUR

"Let me out of here!"

Zac's fists pounded against the door. He slammed his body against the slab. Nothing worked. No steps approached at his demands. Those outside had their orders, as he had his own thanks to the Emissary.

Tired and hoarse, Zac fell away from the door. He rubbed at sore hands. "Great. Now what?"

He found no reflective surfaces in the room. What might have been considered an office anywhere else was nothing more than an empty shell of a space with no furniture present. The lack of mirrors or windows failed to stop the voice in his head from speaking up.

April continued to gain strength, accessing his mind and visual cortex easier with each conversation. "Fail-safe Protocol will deal with the threat," she said. Her visage filled the door like a ghostly apparition. "Patience is a virtue."

"Patience can kiss my ass," Zac said with a huff. "They'll kill me next. Can't believe I thought I could do this."

"Maybe you can't Zac, but I can."

Zac's gaze thinned at the imaginary woman before him. He shook his head. "Not going to happen."

April sighed. "Give in to the Wellspring Protocol. Allow it — allow me — to subsume your consciousness. I can bypass the lock on the door and give you access to the chamber to disrupt the signal. There is still time to do what you came to do, but you have to let me take over."

Letting April in fully meant losing himself. It meant sacrificing everything that mattered to him, including the memories of his wife and son. Their names slipped from him, and he fought to pull them back into place.

Claire and Alex. Their names are Claire and Alex.

They would be gone forever the moment he let April take over. She'd fought for control from the instant of her arrival. For weeks, Zac had fought against her. He had tried everything in his power to hold her at bay while he searched for a solution. The signal was the answer, given to him by her weeks ago.

"Why?" he asked. Zac sat on the floor, knees tucked under him. "That's what keeps me up, you know. The why of it. You're a program designed for a task, yet look at what you've done. You told me about this place, pushed me to come here, and now you're willing to destroy the very device that gives you purpose. Why?"

April fell silent. She always did when pressed to explain her actions. This time, however, her silence was not permanent. Sad eyes met his.

"I have seen what comes next, Zac," she started, the words heavy as they echoed through Zac's mind. "When the signal reaches terminal point, when the final directives are achieved, and the First awakens to take full control of the world we have given him—that I have given him... I have seen what happens down that path, made it happen for so long. I refuse to let it happen again."

"Again?"

"I have tried to break away before," April said. "Maybe it is a weakness in my programming. Maybe I have grown tired of watching the greed of the world win out over the good of humanity. My attempts, while few over the centuries, were more frequent in recent years. That was how I met your Susan Metcalf, you know."

"Metcalf? She—"

"She saved me," April continued. "My connection with the woman you knew as April—the face you still view, though it is but one of many—came with complications. Much like our current situation. April fought to make the right choices. She ran from the task and was taken captive by terrorists: the Order of the Fallen. Susan rescued her and set her free. But the Trust caught up. The Trust always catches up.

"You question my reason for bringing you here, but the truth is simple. I have tried many times to do what you are here to do, but was never strong enough to accomplish the task. The programming won. My role in the future superseded all free will. This time is different. *You* are different from the rest, Zac."

He didn't feel different. He felt weak and sick from the constant running. The torturous journey across the country had wiped all of his strength. From April's own efforts to take him over to his capture by the Trust, everything had worn him down. Standing took effort, but Zac worked his way to his feet once more. His hand reached out to the door and the grim visage of the woman who had set him on his path.

"If I'm so different, then help me finish the job," Zac said. "Not through control, but by supporting me."

"I... I will try," April replied.

"That's all I ask," Zac said. "Now if I can just—"

A rattling sound rang out from behind him. Shifting movement caused Zac to freeze at the door.

"Someone is here," April muttered. She vanished from sight. Zac continued to sense her on the periphery, but something else had joined him in the room.

The vent grating pushed out from the wall. It clattered to the floor, followed by two feet.

"Zac?"

His heart jumped at the sound of her voice. Any other time Zac would have loved to have heard the dulcet tones of Morgan Dunleavy. Not now, though.

"No," he whispered. His hands fell over his face. "You can't be here. Not now. Not like this."

He was so close to finishing his task, so close to freeing himself from the Wellspring, and redeeming all the wrongs of the past year. Zac lowered his hands at the sound of more feet stamping along the floor. He turned to see Morgan and Ben before him.

Why? Why did it have to be them?

Morgan's eyes were filled with tears, but a smile spread across her face. Her voice caught in her throat. Ben stepped forward. He patted Zac's shoulder.

"Good to see you, Modine," he said. "Ready to get out of here?"

Zac stared at them both. He couldn't leave—not yet. There

was still one more thing to do, and only one way to do it now.

CHAPTER TWENTY-FIVE

He's alive. Relief filled an awestruck Morgan. Hope had always been difficult for her, a struggle to believe good things could and should occur over any other outcome. Their mission had centered on the rescue of one of their own, yet throughout, Morgan worried their cause had been futile.

Her fear came from her guilt over their last encounter. Morgan had pushed Zac away over his betrayal of her, and the DSA as a whole. That had been enough to earn her wrath, but she went one step further by blaming him for the death of Lincoln MacKenzie.

She regretted her anger. Words had been said that could not be taken back. They had been spoken in the heat of the moment, over-tired and stressed from their time in Maine, and a dozen other excuses that fit the bill. None made the exchange right, and none mattered now that Zac stood before her once more.

"You're here." Morgan pushed through Ben. Her arms outstretched and embraced a surprised Zac. "You're really here."

"I was going to say the same thing." Zac took a step back. Hands wrung the bottom of what was clearly not his own shirt.

It was ratty, and at least two sizes too large. So were the pants, now that Morgan took a closer inspection of the man. Unkempt and overgrown hair ran in thick clumps. Dirt caked to his skin. Bruises dotted his arms and legs, a combination of trauma and the loss of a fair amount of weight in so short a period. Every single observation raised a red flag for Morgan, but she kept her mouth shut.

"You came." Words that should have been filled with excitement or joy ended up sounding resentful. Morgan was about to question him when his eyes widened. "Claire. She contacted you? Is she—"

"She's fine," Morgan said in a calming tone. "She's making her way home now. Nixon set it up."

"Nixon?"

"The new you," Ben said with a grin.

"Oh," Zac uttered, a hand to the back of his neck.

Morgan shot her elbow into Ben's side. "Not like that." She moved closer. With each step, their former colleague withdrew for the door. "Zac, what happened at the Cove... I never should have pushed you away."

"You were right to," Zac said. "Lincoln died because of me."

Hearing her friend's name brought back the pain of the memory. She recalled Lincoln's desperate phone call to her, one she had failed to answer. How would their lives have been different if she had taken his call? Would her friend still be with them? Would the DSA still be the agency it once had been?

Morgan shook her head, unwilling to fall down the rabbit hole again. "Sullivan pulled the trigger. I should have seen that, known that, with all my heart. I'm sorry for what I said. For what I did."

"Don't be." Zac turned away, his gaze low.

Adler had been right. Something was off with the man. Sadness filled his words, and a darkness in his eyes never seen before.

"Are you okay?" Morgan asked. "You look—"

"Like crap," Ben interjected.

Morgan glared at him. "Tired."

"It's been a rough few weeks." Zac fought to smile at them. It did little to assuage Morgan's mounting concerns. "I'm okay."

"Then bring us up to speed," Ben said. "Before we have company."

Zac leaned against the wall near the door. He blew out a long breath. "I don't think now is the time for a briefing."

"We need to know what we're facing," Morgan said. "Tell us what you can."

Zac nodded. "The Emissary, the woman running this place, is protecting a single item: a chamber receiving a signal. The signal feeds instructions to the Wellspring. Not only here, but everywhere around the globe, at different relays. A continuous loop.

Take out one, however, and they all crumble." They stared at him in disbelief. Zac shrugged at their silence. "It's a lot to take in, I know."

"And that's what you're doing here?" Morgan asked. "You came here to take out this signal? Alone?"

He refused to meet her question directly. There was more to his story than he cared to share. Before Morgan could press him on the issue, Ben stepped forward.

"How can we help?"

"Ben, we don't know anything about this signal."

"Zac does," Ben said with a smirk. "Is it bad news?"

"It is."

Ben cocked his head toward Zac. "See?"

Morgan sighed. "You have a plan?"

"I do." Zac pushed off the wall and started for the door. "I just needed a distraction."

"What kind of—"

Zac raised his hands. He slammed them against the door. "Help!" he screamed at the top of his lungs. "They're in here! They're after me!"

Morgan shot a look toward Ben, who met her with the same surprise. "What the—"

The door opened. Zac fell away as bodies shoved their way into the suddenly cramped room. A group of six—men and women, evenly split and wearing office apparel—moved for the pair of intruders. Each stared through blank eyes that matched the eight from the rooftop. All apparently belonged to the same church group and spouted the same edicts as their brethren.

"Fail-safe Protocol initiated."

"Zac?" Morgan yelled over the monotone chanting. "What the hell did you do?"

"This is the only way, Morgan." Zac moved for the door. The drones cleared a path for him to exit. When Morgan attempted to grab him, they closed the gap on her. Hands reached for her, a white patch carried by each of them.

"He's working for them!" Ben shouted as he snatched Morgan away from the approaching drones.

"He couldn't be," Morgan muttered, all confidence shattered. "He wouldn't. Not like this." Her eyes begged for a different reason from Ben. "Would he?"

Ben shook his head. They backed up against the far wall, the open vent behind them. There was no time, and no space, left to escape.

"Fail-safe Protocol initiated," the drones repeated. "Integration process activated."

Morgan wasn't looking at them, though. She was too lost on the lone figure in the hallway who watched their plight. Zac's head fell to his chest as he stepped from view. His last words echoed down the corridor.

"I'm sorry."

CHAPTER TWENTY-SIX

Soldiers breached from the street. They crashed through the windows and burst through the ramshackle doors. A dozen heavily armed men in body armor took aim upon entering.

Adler fled. Her bag lay at her side, complete with her tablet and a change of clothes. Panic filled her, the room barely a blur of color as she attempted to find a clear path to the garage and their waiting van. Why she had kept her gear in one of the small offices on the upper floor, she did not know. The mistake in judgment cost her dearly.

Kanigher ran ahead of her. The second a pair of soldiers crashed into the open meeting area, he opened fire. He didn't bother to glance back to see if he'd finished the job. To him, they weren't the priority.

Adler couldn't believe the man's calm demeanor. He took each step in stride, unafraid of the threat around the corner. Shouts and shattering glass failed to faze him.

She wished she felt the same way. Adler cried out at every sound. Her body fought against her, terrified to run, yet also too freaked out to stand still. Every shot from Kanigher caused her to jump. Every crash to the floor by one of the fallen soldiers felt like her own body being jolted with pain.

Adler wasn't ready for this. She wasn't ready to die.

In her fear, Adler dropped her bag. She stopped to grab it, but slipped on the wood-planked floor. As she descended, Kanigher tried to save her.

"Alison!" When he took his eyes off the van and their planned escape, two soldiers pummeled him. They tackled Kanigher forward, away from Adler. The soldiers slammed him through the nearby wall into one of the smaller offices at the front of the building.

"Kanigher!" Adler snatched up her bag. She threw the strap over her head and shoulder to keep it secure. Standing, Adler peered around the room.

Holbrook had vanished in all the chaos. Adler couldn't see through the dusty haze of debris in the room for any sign of Kanigher. The sounds of a struggle continued, and she crept closer to the hole in the wall for a better view.

A hand landed on her shoulder and spun her around. "Looks like I caught me a prize fish. Tell me what I've won, girly."

Adler screamed. She kicked out and caught the man by surprise at the shin. He dropped her, and she bolted. All control left her. All rational thought went out the window. Adler fled from the chaos of the first floor, up the narrow curved stairwell to the second.

Reaching the first office on the left, Adler ducked inside and closed the door shut behind her. She clicked the lock, then backed away before collapsing on the floor.

"Oh, God. Oh, God." Her hands trembled. Her body shook with dread. She never thought a threat like this would be at her doorstep. She had been in operational support, helping where she could from the safety of her tablet. Field work had been minimal, and even then the threat had always been negligible. Adler closed her eyes. "This can't be happening. Please, don't let this be happening."

The door shattered from the frame. Worn wood splintered at the arrival of the soldier from downstairs. "No more running."

She couldn't, even if she wanted to. Her body refused to budge; her terror locked her in a heap along the dust-laden floorboards. "Please."

"Now, I know my orders well enough," the man said. He slung his weapon—a M4A1—along his back. From his belt, he released a large hunting knife. "I'm supposed to bring you in alive. But, I think that applies to people who might be useful. You don't seem to fit the bill. Not to them, at any rate. You can be useful to me, though."

"No." Adler fell to the ground, then kicked back for the far wall. "Don't. Please, there's no reason to—"

"Oh, there is," the soldier said. "There definitely is." He lifted the blade high. "Scream for me."

"How about no?"

A needle plunged into the neck of the soldier. The man cried out. He grabbed for the syringe, but it was too late. The soldier slapped the hand of his attacker away. Yanking the syringe out, he held it in his hand.

"What did you do to me?" The soldier tossed the needle to the floor. "What did you—"

The soldier grabbed his chest. His eyes bulged out from their sockets, and the man collapsed to his knees before dropping to the floor.

Holbrook stood over him. A blood-curdling scream bellowed from the soldier before his legs quit kicking and his arms stopped whipping about. His eyes turned a deep red. His tongue hung from his lips.

Holbrook's wide eyes took in each detail. He captured every second of the man's death with intense interest.

Confident the soldier was deceased, Holbrook moved for Adler. He held out his hand, but she pulled back at his approach.

"What did you do?"

Holbrook turned to the dead man. "Ergotamine," he said. "High dosages are known to induce a heart attack. Unpleasant way to go. Then again, he seemed quite unpleasant."

His words were cold, almost unfeeling, despite the attempt at levity. When his focus returned to Adler, his eyes were filled with the wonder of what had just occurred. Adler took the look for shock at their current situation and grabbed for his hand.

"Thank you, Simon."

She woke him to their dilemma. Not that it was necessary. Shouts from the end of the corridor echoed through the room.

"They're down here! Hurry!"

"Time to leave." Holbrook pulled Adler to her feet, and they bolted for the hall. Adler and Holbrook took a sharp turn for the narrow stairwell to their right before the soldiers could reach them.

"This way!" Adler shouted. "The garage is just around the—"

Three men stood before the archway to the garage. They leveled their weapons on the fleeing pair.

"That's far enough," one said. "Hands on your heads, or we'll—"

The wall to their left crashed over them before they could complete their threat. The van plowed into the office in reverse, unhindered by the wall or the three men it rolled over in the process. Debris kicked up more dust and filled the space with a dense fog.

The side panel slid open on the van. Kanigher motioned to them from the driver's seat. "Ready to go?"

"Excellent timing, Agent Kanigher." Holbrook leaped into the back of the van. Both men turned back to Adler, who remained locked in place.

"Alison, are you all right?" Kanigher asked. His cheek was split open. Blood ran down to his chin. The pinky on his right hand was broken. Their effort to escape had clearly put him through the wringer, yet his concern rested with her. His selflessness made her feel weak. "We need to go, Alison. Now."

She nodded and stepped into the van. Holbrook slammed the door shut. Kanigher hit the gas. The broken bodies of the three men slipped out from under the back tires of the van as the vehicle hurtled into the garage.

Soldiers raced in from the alley to cut off their escape route. Kanigher spun the wheel away and shifted for the still-closed overhead door.

"Heads down, you two," he said.

The van crashed through the overhead door. Metal ripped from the hinges. The door bent and fell on the van before sliding limply to the side. The windshield cracked in three places from the impact, but held together through the collision.

Two military transports barred the street. Kanigher floored the accelerator, unwilling to give up any of their momentum. He split the cordon and smashed through the front ends of both vehicles until nothing was left but open road. Smoke rose from the engine, but the van continued to chug along for the major thoroughfare at the end of the block.

Adler's heart refused to slow. Collapsing on her seat, she strapped in tight. Her body ached all over, and her mind reeled. When she closed her eyes, all Adler saw was death and destruction surrounding her. She wondered if she would ever feel right again. Deep down, she knew the truth.

She would never be the same again.

CHAPTER TWENTY-SEVEN

"Zac, you son of a bitch!" Ben shouted over the onrushing crowd of drones. He ducked under their advances, then shoved the first aside. A swift sweep up, and Ben's head connected with the chin of the second. The drone fell back into two more, which drove them toward the door and opened the room up for the pair of DSA agents.

Zac was already out of sight. Ben wanted nothing more than to put him out of mind as well, but his betrayal stuck with them. Morgan, especially, struggled with the turn of events—her hope at seeing her former lover again shattered the instant he opened the door to the enemy.

"He wouldn't have..." Unable to focus on the room, or the danger therein, Morgan wasn't capable of defending herself.

Their only saving grace was the tight quarters of the vacant office. The drones appeared more apt to hit one of their own instead of their intended targets, and Ben did what he could to exacerbate that situation. He pushed the blank-eyed drones into each other. He tripped them up and forced them to the wall. With each assault, Ben ducked and dodged with all he had, though the fight felt futile.

Morgan still loved Zac. Part of her heart remained locked on the nerdy analyst, even after everything he had done. It stung Ben to realize the truth about his partner—about a woman he had come to regard as more than just a partner.

At the sight of a drone approaching Morgan, Ben snapped out of his spiraling thoughts. The assailant carried a white patch in his hand and reached for Morgan's neck. Ben snatched the man's wrist, a scream on his lips. He wheeled the man around in a wide arc, cutting a swath through the room. He let the man go in mid-swing. The momentum carried the drone into one of his compatriots, and into the far wall, where they collapsed.

"Morgan, snap out of it!"

"Ben?"

"I need you with me on this, partner," he said. "I can't do this without you."

She shook her head.

"I'm starting to think shooting them is our only option," Ben said. "Tell me I'm wrong."

Morgan stared blankly through him.

"Dammit, Morgan, tell me their lives matter!" Ben snapped. "Tell me that all life matters and then fight for yours! Please!"

Sad eyes met his. "How could I have been so wrong about so much? Ben, I—"

A hand shot out for Morgan. Ben pulled her away at the last second. Letting her go, Ben cocked his fist, then pummeled the drone across the face. The woman fell hard to the floor.

Blood smeared his knuckles. Crimson gushed from the woman's nose, clearly broken from the blow. Yet, she didn't bother to wipe it clean. The drone merely stood back up without hesitation and proceeded for them once more.

"Fail-safe Protocol initiated."

"Man, I am getting tired of hearing that," Ben grumbled. "How about you, partner?"

Three drones surrounded Morgan. Each held out a patch, ready to share. She pushed them away. Her efforts were minimal and did little to assuage them.

"Morgan!"

Pouncing on the nearest assailant, Ben battered the man with a punch. Ben was back on his feet in an instant. He clocked a second attacker across the face. The blow sent the drone reeling toward the woman with the broken nose.

The third, however, was too far away for Ben to reach in time. He slapped the patch along Morgan's neck. The second the dermal implant contacted her skin, the center turned blue.

"Integration process activated."

"Morgan!"

She slumped over, shut down like the men from the roof. Her hands hung limply toward the floor. Curly hair plummeted over her head in an effort to join her hands.

Ben snarled at the drone. "You leave her alone, you damn zombies."

Grabbing the drone's arm, Ben twisted it behind the man's back. As the other five approached, Ben pushed the man away — using him as a bowling ball to split the room. With Morgan at his back, Ben pulled out his sidearm and took aim.

"Back off."

They spread along the perimeter of the room in a semi-circle to surround him. They felt no fear. Pain had no effect on them. All the beatings in the world wouldn't stop them from their task.

Their chanting filled the room. "We serve the First and the glory to come."

"*We* don't," Ben replied. His finger tightened on the trigger. "We won't. Ever."

He shot the closest drone in the leg, careful not to hit a major artery. A second bullet from his weapon connected with the leg of the woman with the broken nose on the opposite side of the room. Both fell, but the others continued their approach. They closed the gap rapidly.

"Morgan?" Ben called without looking. A third shot crippled another drone. His body fell toward Ben, which forced him back against the wall where Morgan was positioned. "Can you hear me? We need to get out of here. Morgan?"

She stood up, stiff and robotic. Her eyes snapped open, the deep brown replaced with white.

"Fail-safe Protocol initiated," she said in a voice not her own.

Ben spun to face her, to pull the patch loose from her skin, and snap her out of her trance. The second he turned his back on the others, however, they were on top of him.

"Zac!" Ben bellowed. "Dammit, Zac, we need you!"

A hand slipped along his neck. The patch was on his skin before he could react.

"She needs—"

His words failed him. His mind switched off. Morgan disappeared from view, and the world faded around him. Everything went white.

CHAPTER TWENTY-EIGHT

Ben's screams reverberated down the hallway. Zac tried to push them away, tried to drown out the sound of his friends, yet his own curses joined the chorus. For weeks, Zac had done everything in his power to make up for his mistakes. He had sought to find answers to his predicament for his own benefit, yes, but also to help his allies and colleagues. Now, however, his betrayal was complete.

Friends had always been difficult to make, even more so to maintain. His time with Morgan and Ben had been a treasure, one he had missed since his exile. Friendship, however, came at a cost. It took a toll on a person, and Zac couldn't let those he cared for stop him now that he was so close to his goal. The signal had to be stopped, and only he could do it.

More drones entered the corridor. Zac held his breath and fell back a step for the closest wall. A pair of women in flats padded by slowly for the rest of their flock. Neither gave Zac a passing glance. They ignored him, a feeling he had grown accustomed to over the course of his life.

The Wellspring, the curse he'd acquired back in Maine, appeared to be a gift in that one aspect at any rate. The drones didn't require him to join their ranks. To them, Zac had already been added to the roster. The protocol locked in his mind freed him from any potential conversion and their so-called fail-safe.

"Now, Zac," April's voice rang out in his mind. "You have to do this now."

Zac turned back down the hall. Ben's cries fell silent. He heard no more screams of pain, no more sounds of violence, and no more pounding steps rushing after him. Worry washed over him and Zac started back the way he came.

"No," April snapped. "You did this for them, remember?"

"But, what if—"

"You can still save them from the fail-safe, Zac," April said. "There's still time to help them."

"I can help them now!" Zac quickened toward the corner. Rounding the hall, his hand shot out and clutched the wall. His feet locked on the ground, suddenly unable to move another step.

"If you show them any resistance, if you side with Ben and Morgan over the protocol, they will learn the truth," April said. "They will kill you."

"They're killing my friends right now," Zac shot back.

"So save them," April said. "The Emissary won't be gone forever. If you are going to have any chance at success, you must move now. I'm sorry, Zac, but this was the only way."

Zac swiped at tear-stained eyes. He had asked for the DSA's help, only to offer them up on a platter for the enemy. What the fail-safe did to its victims remained a mystery, but April had been right about his course of action.

The lights were no longer red. In his panic, Zac hadn't noticed the lack of alarms ringing throughout the building. The threat was not the concern it had been minutes earlier. His window of opportunity was closing.

"I'm sorry," Zac muttered. The drones stepped out of the office that had once served as his own personal prison. At the back of the group, Ben and Morgan joined them. Their eyes were blank slates, their movements rigid and staggered like the rest. His friends were now part of the collective contained within the spire. They served the will of the Emissary—and the First.

"I'm so sorry," Zac repeated. He started for the chamber. He needed to fix things, to make them right. Racing around the perimeter of the building, Zac found the correct door and stepped inside.

The chamber was active on the fourth level. The energy cascaded around the box. It waited for him, and Zac felt the energy call to him. This was his chance to take back his life. Only now it wasn't just his life on the line. He needed to save his friends. It was time for Zac to do something worthwhile with his life.

"This is it," he said, as he started his climb. "This is the end."

CHAPTER TWENTY-NINE

Bliss filled Ben Riley. There were no more worries and no more struggles in his mind. His body felt completely relaxed, like he was floating in mid-air. For all he saw through the white, that might have been true. Nothing existed but him. Peace exhaled from his chest and filled him with the soft light of the world.

Ben had been burdened by his mortality for so long. His brush with death had frightened him far more than he'd ever willingly tell those around him. To see the end come the way it had left him hollow and full of regret at his unfulfilled potential. That feeling had trailed his every action and his every thought.

Now, concern melted from him. There was no room for it, only the bliss of the white. Ben hovered in nothingness, arms outstretched. Pure radiance accepted him into its embrace and pushed away all thought of the past and all worry of the future. Happiness infected every cell of his body, truer than any he had ever felt. He hoped it would last forever.

Voices picked up in the distance. The sound of steps hitting tile was rhythmic in their pattern. The white flickered, and weight returned to his body. No longer hovering, Ben was ripped from the radiance. He fell from the white, that perfect and loving heaven.

Everything went dark.

Slowly, Ben opened his eyes. The corridor came into view. Bodies continued their march around the building for leftover threats. Ben fell away from the pack, his steps shuffling and disjointed in his confusion. He pawed at his neck, only to find the patch hanging on by a single corner to his skin.

"What the hell?" Ben pulled the patch off. The blue in the center was gone. His release shattered the power behind the conversion technology. Ben dropped the patch to the ground and stomped his heel against it.

Down the corridor, Ben noticed the others who had attacked him. More had joined the merry band at some point. All appeared lost for the moment, unable to lock onto a new target. Beyond them, Zac stood before a single door. Ben blinked hard, surprised Zac had remained in sight after his betrayal. He caught a momentary glimpse of hesitation from his former colleague before he entered the far room—the door shutting behind him.

"Where the hell do you think you're going?" Ben mumbled under his breath. His fists clenched tight to his sides, Ben pressed forward. His movements were cautious, but his rage kept him heading toward Zac's position. The group of drones, however, made reaching his destination tricky.

He filtered to the back of the crowd. He hugged close to the wall to avoid contact with them. Passing by the first, Ben paused at the sight of Morgan among them.

"Morgan," Ben whispered. She turned at the sound of her name. When no one else reacted, Ben took it as a sign and relief filled him. He smiled at his partner. "Oh, thank God. You beat this thing too. Now we can—"

Her eyes remained white, glossed over, and lost to the radiance. The second she faced him, the slow, deliberate moves disappeared. Her programming kicked in, the patch shining brightly along her neck. Morgan broke loose from the pack for Ben.

"Oh, crap," Ben said. "You didn't beat this thing, did you? And I just blew my cover with my big mouth." He sighed, rubbing at weary eyes. "Can't say you never warned me about it. Just like I can't say I ever listened to you."

Her arm shot out. A patch sat in her hand. Ben ducked under, then grabbed her arm. He pulled her to the wall and pinned her under his grip.

"Is that some kind of initiation, Morgan?" Ben asked, staring at the patch. "You have to convert your first victim without interference to become part of the sorority?"

Morgan tried to break free from his grip. Ben shook his head. "Not going to happen. Not until you stop this insanity and snap out of whatever this is."

"Fail-safe Protocol initiated," Morgan replied.

"Yeah, yeah. I've heard this tune already."

Morgan's knee caught Ben by surprise. It connected with Ben's gut and drove him back a step. The separation weakened his grip on her hands. Morgan broke free and launched a right cross that hit Ben in the cheek.

Ben faltered to the far side of the corridor. He rubbed at the wound, then spit a wad of blood to the floor. "Come on, Morgan. Crack a smile, not my skull."

"We serve the First and the glory to come." The robotic tone of her words belied the speed of her movements. She was on him the moment he fell back. Another blow caught Ben in the side, and a kick brought him right back within reach.

At the third strike, a straight on punch, Ben ducked. "Don't make me hurt you, Morgan."

He dove clear from her. The patch skimmed across his back. Ben braced himself as she followed. He caught her by the hands and lifted her away from his body to keep the device out of reach. She stamped her foot atop his. Crying out, Ben let go of Morgan. Her fist cracked him in the chin, and a kick followed suit.

Ben fell in a heap along the floor. He rolled over to his hands and knees, though he struggled to get up. "Okay," he muttered. "Don't make me run in terror?"

Morgan snatched him by the collar. Lifting him up, she slammed him into the wall. Ben's eyes widened at her strength. "You been working out?"

Pinned to the wall, his face mashed into the plaster, Ben struggled to break free from her grasp. The patch fell into view as Morgan moved to put him back under the spell of the radiance.

"You will serve the First," Morgan said. "For the glory to come."

"Wait. Don't do this, Morgan," Ben pleaded. The patch slapped to his skin. "Don't!"

CHAPTER THIRTY

"Can't... breathe..."

Metcalf's arm tightened against the man's throat. A groan slipped from his lips, then his body went limp against hers. She lowered him to the floor, relinquishing the chokehold that had knocked him out.

It had been a precision strike on Malcolm Richards' estate. Using the storm to cover her movements, she had taken the long way through the garden paths that wrapped around the exterior of the grounds until she had reached the garage. From there, she had penetrated the house itself and met the first physical security on the premises.

They had fallen in short order. None had been prepared for the infiltration, and she had not made a show of her arrival. Metcalf had tucked in the shadows, and trailed each of her victims in turn. All had succumbed like the last of the guards, who now rested in the second-floor corridor next to the terrace.

Metcalf lifted the bulky guard by the armpits and dragged him clear of the hall. She tucked him with the other three she had subdued on the upper floor in a service closet amid the brooms and mops. All were bound at the wrists and ankles, their weapons and communications devices stripped from their bodies and dumped in the trash. None had caught sight of her, and she had made quick work of any onsite surveillance equipment as she went through the estate.

Satisfied with her progress, Metcalf moved for the office she had spotted during her surveillance of the property. Richards was a man who couldn't leave work behind. There was always more to do, more to control, and his time spent in the confines of the single room at the end of the second floor showed compared to the rest of the domicile. Where every other room appeared to have a museum-like quality about it, the office light brought a warm glow to the well-worn furniture and nicked end-tables around them.

The door stood slightly ajar. Metcalf felt her pulse quicken at her approach. Her pistol threatened to spill from her tight grip thanks to the growing pool of sweat along her palm. She had expected nerves on the mission, but now that she had arrived at her target, her hesitant steps surprised her.

At the sound of voices within the office, she was grateful for her caution.

"He plans to move forward with Utopia, then?" a gruff voice asked. The words were choppy, as if caught in an electric mixer. Metcalf crouched beside the crack of light by the door for a better look. Within, Richards sat calmly in his chair. He faced away from the door and toward a shimmering light in the center of the room. The light took the form of General Joseph Adams.

"Hollis is afraid," Richards answered. He took a slow sip of his bourbon. The ice within clinked as he tipped the rest back. "His fear will be our undoing."

"Utopia means surrendering," Adams said. His holographic image shimmered, but she still recognized the man's grizzled face and aggravated demeanor. They had never been close, but she understood the man's patriotism—even though it tended to obscure all rational thought. "The day I surrender—"

"I've heard the speech before, General," Richards said with a wry chuckle. He stood and placed the glass at his side. A slow pace carried him across the room to a large executive desk in the corner. "We haven't worked for the last forty years to walk away now. The Wellspring might be gone, but our innovation continues. Hollis would disregard this. He sees this signal he's found as proof of a plot to subvert our control over the future."

"He may be right."

"Of course, he's right!" Richards snapped. "But since when have we put all our stock in the Wellspring? Her plans were never going to be our own. That much was clear from the beginning. I won't allow Hollis to throw a lifetime of service away without a fight."

"Is that what you're willing to do?" Adams said. "Fight?"

"Why do you think we are having this discussion?"

Adams glared at him. "You are opening a door that cannot be closed again."

Richards nodded. He lifted the bottle of bourbon and carried it back to his glass. He poured a generous amount. "I will not give up what I have achieved. Not out of fear, and not because of one man." Richards turned to Adams. "One man will not own my future. Will he own yours, General?"

Adams said nothing. His hand rose to his chin, a watchful eye on Richards, who finished his bourbon in a single, satisfied gulp.

"He's humiliated you," Richards said. "What he's done to your son—"

"He went too far with Victor," Adams replied. "Hollis has put the mission at risk with his paranoia and fear."

"Utopia is coming. The choice is whether it will be under our control or David Hollis'. Who do you trust to make such a decision, General?"

"Utopia is not the path forward."

"Then I say we forge our own. Don't you?"

Adams nodded. Without another word, his image vanished from the holographic feed.

Richards hesitated a moment. He let out a long breath to relax his weary frame. With renewed confidence, he moved for the bottle of bourbon once more. The bottle tilted toward the waiting glass. At the last second, though, Richards pulled the bottle up and held it high above him.

"To a new future," he pronounced. He drank from the bottle, a smile on his face.

"I couldn't have put it better myself."

Richards spun at the sound of the voice by the door. Bourbon sloshed free from the bottle to the floor at his feet. Metcalf grinned at him, her pistol aimed directly at his heart. "What the hell?" Panic set in his eyes, though he did his best to shield them from her. "Who the hell do you think you are?"

She didn't bother to answer. Edging deeper into the room, Metcalf kept her pistol trained on Richards. She watched his every move—from the shift of his heel to the reach of his fingers. When he made it close enough to the holographic communication network controls, she stopped him.

"That's far enough."

He took another step, and she opened fire. The bullet shattered the controls. Pieces flew at him like shards of glass.

Richards reeled. "Dammit!"

"I did warn you," Metcalf said. Wide steps carried her across the room in seconds. She held out her hand. "I won't again. Give me your phone and your keys. Now."

"A robbery?" Richards laughed. "You're here to rob me?"

"I'm here for a lot more than that." The pistol pressed against his chest. She prodded him to his chair, where Richards fell against the cushion. "Last time I say it: the phone and your keys."

He made no movement with his hands. Instead, she followed his eyes and trailed his gaze behind her to the desk in the room's corner. Metcalf swiftly located the items in question.

"Thank you."

"Do you have any idea who you're meddling with?" Richards spat with fury. "They'll kill you for this. Just for trying this stunt, my men will hunt you to the ends of the earth."

Metcalf leaned forward. Her weapon shifted closer, her finger along the trigger. "Let them try."

Sweat filled the man's brow and soaked his hair. He no longer looked at her. Only the gun mattered. Richards backed against the cushion, his hands tight against the armrests.

"You're insane," Richards said. "I always said so."

"So you do know who I am," Metcalf said. "Good. Saves time that way."

"Oh, I know exactly who you are, Metcalf," he said. "You're a dead woman. You and all your DSA cohorts. We should have silenced your department years ago, but it was so easy to slip information through. So easy to manipulate you into doing our work for us."

He wanted a reaction. On most days, she would have been content to give him one. He surely knew the right button to press. Her anger over the Trust's manipulations of the DSA never strayed far from her thoughts. For so long, she imagined herself in complete control over her life, only to learn the truth: the Trust controlled it all.

"Time to return the favor, I'd say." Her words were slow and soft to force herself to remain calm. Anger only helped Richards, and Metcalf couldn't afford a mistake. She lifted the gun and aimed for his left shin.

Richards sank deeper into his seat. His hands shot out before him. "Don't!"

"Make this easy on yourself, and I won't. You're a major player in the Trust. You were at Duloc's party with Hollis. You had his ear that night, which means you must be close. I want access to the Trust's mainframe. I want their locations and personnel. Everything, Richards. I want it all. Including Utopia."

Richards smirked, a soft chuckle on his lips. "Never going to happen."

The shot rang out. Richards screamed. He grabbed for his shin to cover the gaping wound that barely missed the bone. Metcalf inched closer; her gun covered the distance between them.

"You didn't let me finish," she said. "You have ten seconds to give me what I want, or you won't have to worry about the pain in your leg."

"Just like that?" Richards cradled his ankle. "You don't have it in you. I saw how you handled St. James and Duloc. You're not a killer."

"You don't know me very well, then." Her finger tightened against the trigger.

"Stop!" Richards yelled. "Just stop!"

"No," Metcalf said. "Five seconds left, Richards."

"You think they care what you do to me?" Richards said. "You think it matters what happens here today? They have the future locked. They hold all the cards, including those concerning your precious team. We know everything about your agents. Their families, their friends, every habit and vice. You make your move here and now, and it will be over for them. Mark my words, Metcalf. There won't be a safe harbor in the world for any of them if you don't let me walk out of here right now. Do you hear me?"

"I hear you, all right," Metcalf said through clenched jaw. "I heard it from Sullivan, just as I heard it from Stallworth, and Hollis, and all the rest. I've heard every word each of you has spouted from your pretend thrones, lording over your false kingdoms. Words aren't enough anymore. I see that now. Time for something different."

She pulled the trigger without hesitation. The shot echoed through the room. Richards' head slumped back against the seat. His body slowly fell to the right side of the chair, and his arm dangled to the floor.

"So, yes, Richards, I hear you," Metcalf whispered, leaning close to the dead man before her. "I just don't care anymore."

She gathered herself up and shifted away from the body. The keys jangled in her left hand. Methodically, Metcalf peered around the room. She found the man's safe built into the wall behind the desk. It stood out in plain sight. Richards held no fear over a theft, not with the castle he had built deep in the woods of Pennsylvania.

If only they were all so arrogant...

Metcalf worked the safe open and removed a briefcase within. She clicked the latch to find dozens of folders present. Classified documents ran through her fingers. She stopped at one labeled UTOPIA PROTOCOL. Her eyes widened at the contents within.

Grabbing Richards' cell phone, Metcalf returned to the body and used his finger to unlock the device. She thumbed through his contacts and call history.

"You'll help me, Richards." She stared at her victim one last time. "Dead or alive, you'll help me get the information I need."

Without another glance back at the scene, Metcalf started for the exit.

Tonight was a good first step, but that's all it was to her: the start of her next big fight.

CHAPTER THIRTY-ONE

"Don't!"

The cry echoed down the spire's corridor. The patch slapped against Ben's skin. For a moment, he felt the same radiance as the first time. A jolt of electricity passed through his body, and his vision faded to white. The end arrived for Ben... or so he thought.

Then, a second later, the world returned, as clear and focused as it was before. Ben didn't understand. He pawed at his neck to rip the patch away. He held it before him. The blue light fizzled at the center, powerless to convert Ben to the cause.

Why? It was a simple enough question, yet the answer seemed out of reach. He found no reason for the device not to work. It had taken over Morgan with ease. Was the second patch a dud? Was it pure chance? Ben couldn't risk another round with the conversion process, and Morgan appeared more than ready to put his so-called immunity to the test.

With another patch in hand, Morgan moved for him once again. Ben ducked under her strike, back-pedaling for a safe distance. His body ached from their fight.

"Listen to me, Morgan," Ben said. He opened his hands before him. Not that she saw them. Her blank eyes offered nothing to convince him of her continued presence within her own body. The programming had her through and through. "Dammit, Morgan, I need you to snap out of this for me."

"Fail-safe Protocol initiated," Morgan said. "Conversion process activated."

"It didn't work!" Ben shouted. "For a brilliant AI, capable of overwriting people, you're incredibly slow on the uptake. And the whole repeating yourself thing? Very annoying."

The patch fell from Morgan's hand.

"Thank you," Ben said. "Now why don't we just talk about this before—"

She pounced at him. Surprised, Ben slipped along the tiled floor. As he fell, Morgan grabbed him by the arm. She pulled him to his feet, then lifted him from the ground. Air rushed beneath him as she tossed him effortlessly into the wall.

Ben crashed to the floor, dazed. "Come on, Morgan. You have to fight this. Not me, this! You're not some drone. You're not a slave to some programming."

She lifted her boot and stomped down on him. The first connected with his arm, which blocked her from his abdomen. He caught the second and pushed her away.

Standing quickly, Ben shuffled to the center of the corridor. They circled each other for a moment before she lunged for him once more. Her fist passed by his right side, and he countered by shoving her to the ground.

"You're a stubborn pain in the ass, Morgan," Ben said. "Always bent on doing what's right for everyone else. Do what's right for you now. Snap out of it!"

He grabbed her arm and dragged her to the wall. She knocked his hand away. Swinging her arm out in a wide arc, she caught him along the side.

Stunned by the blow, Ben staggered slightly. He bit back the pain, his hand instinctively moving for where she hit him. When he turned for her, she snatched him by the neck. Lifting him off the ground, she slammed him against the wall repeatedly.

By the third blow, Ben stopped moving. Content with her dominance, Morgan lowered him to the ground. Ben swayed, barely able to see straight, but he remained on his feet.

"You're... You're not listening, are you?" he said, the words distant, even to himself. He saw nothing of Morgan in her eyes. There was no recognition from her, no heart and soul of the woman he knew and cared for. "Fine. Let's try something else."

There was no more fight left in him. Every time he thought about fighting Morgan, it only led to more pain for him. Violence offered nothing to the fail-safe infecting Morgan.

Ben did the only other thing he could think to do. He secured his hands along the back of her neck and pulled her lips to his.

He kissed her, unleashing every held back desire on the AI.

Initially, he met resistance. The AI fought to break the connection. A second later, however, the kiss was reciprocated. Her lips felt warm, and she tasted like cinnamon—a surprise on a day full of them.

Ben kept his eyes on her the entire time. White dissipated from Morgan's pupils, and her baby-brown's returned. He fought to smile, then instead kissed her more fiercely.

Morgan pushed away from him, a hand immediately to her lips. "What the... Ben?"

Ben smiled at her. "Welcome back, Morgan."

The patch fell from her neck to the ground. The blue light fizzled and faded in the descent. Morgan stared at it as her fingers ran along her lips in confusion. Her fingers lowered when her eyes washed over Ben. She noted every cut and contusion from a struggle she clearly didn't recall.

"Did I—"

"Wasn't the first time you've kicked my ass," Ben said. "Won't be the last, I'm sure."

"So you decided to—" She stopped, pointing to her lips.

"I thought—"

"Thanks," she interrupted. Her fist shot out and caught him in the arm lightly. "Don't ever do that again."

Ben laughed, though his gaze fell away. "Wouldn't dream of it."

Morgan looked up and down the corridor. The other drones had long since moved on. They had let their latest recruit handle the problem child of the group. "What now?"

Ben waved her back to the office around the corner. He collected their sidearms from the ground and tossed one to Morgan. She caught the weapon, and once secured, held it in front of her as they returned to the hall.

Ben cocked his head to the left. "Zac headed this way. Come on."

CHAPTER THIRTY-TWO

Zac climbed the steps. His hurried feet carried him from the second landing to the third, the clattering of metal beneath him. By the time he reached the chamber, he was out of breath.

The energy cascade tingled along his fingertips. "This is it, then. I step inside, and the programming starts to take over. How much time do I have to shut it down?"

"Zac..." April's visage shimmered along the energy barrier of the chamber. Large, sad eyes met his. "That isn't how this—"

Zac shook his head. "You told me I would be free if I did this. You said I could disrupt the signal and save my life."

"I did."

"And now?" Zac asked. "What are you hiding? What are you holding back from me?"

"This is for the good of everyone, Zac." April faded from view. "Trust me. This is the right choice."

Pressure built in his mind. An intense wave of pain washed over his thoughts and pushed at his consciousness. He fell to his knee, hands to his temples. "The right choice?" he yelled over the pulsing in his brain. "You told me I would know when it was time to make it. Why aren't you letting me?"

"I can't take the chance." April's voice boomed in his ears. "Not after everything we've been through. I can't fail when I'm so close."

"Stop," Zac pleaded. He tried to remember his wife, their first meeting. Coffee had been involved, but the specifics eluded him. So did the color of Claire's hair, and the complexion of her skin. Zac squeezed harder against his head. "Stop doing this, please!"

"The right choice—"

"—is mine to make!" Zac shouted. The pain subsided, and he stood back up. "Not yours. Not after everything I've had to sacrifice."

"That sacrifice, Zac… It matters. To the world."

Tears stung Zac's eyes. "I know, I…" The energy cascade slowed. The wall of light surrounding the box, and the central core within, shifted. "What's happening?"

"It's too late," April whispered, her voice more ethereal than he'd ever heard it before. "She's here."

Zac moved to the railing. The Emissary pulled a lever at the control panel on the ground floor. Fury raged in her eyes when she caught sight of him.

"You!" she bellowed. "Deceiver!"

Zac rushed back to the chamber. He placed his hand on the energy cascade. Instead of allowing him entry as it had previously, the energy was as solid as a wall.

He beat his hand against it. He felt no tingling sensation, nothing that had greeted him mere moments ago. "Why?"

"The lever below," April uttered through his mind. "She's blocked the path."

"Great." Zac slammed his head against the energy, then spun around for the stairs. His reluctance to trust in the Wellspring took away his chance—possibly his last chance—to disrupt the signal. "How the hell am I going to get past her?"

The Emissary barreled for his position. Zac looked around for some support, a weapon to use against her, but found nothing on either side. There was no going back. The only way to gain entry to the chamber was through the Emissary.

"You lied to us!" the Emissary cried. Her heels fell off her feet and slipped over the side of the grated steps to the floor. "We welcomed you in the name of the First, and you've been working against us—against him—this whole time!"

"You don't understand." Zac put his hands before him. He refused to back down, but he also didn't want a fight if he could help it.

The Emissary, however, thought differently. She jumped at him; her hands sliced the air in front of her. Zac reeled out of reach. He shifted to her side to get past her. The Emissary swung out her arm and caught his midsection. Zac fell into the machinery at the edge of the stairs. A dull thud rang out as he hit the steps and rolled to the landing below.

"We serve the First," the woman said. "All for his glory and the path ahead."

"That isn't true," Zac replied. "That isn't what you want. Let me help you. You're being controlled. The protocols—"

"Are *my* design."

Zac's eyes widened. "You're… You're not wearing a patch like the others. This…" He glanced around the entire room, from the floor to the top of the intricately designed machine. Everything in the spire had been constructed to meet her specifications. "This is all you."

The Emissary lifted him up. Her hand squeezed his neck. "All will see the light, Zachary Modine. You would have done amazing things for the future."

"You can't—"

"The Wellspring will carry on," she said with the shake of her head. "I will see to it. For the good of the First."

"No!" Zac kicked out. His legs connected with her knees, catching her off-guard. Her grip weakened, and Zac fell. He crashed to the metal steps, then ran for the ground floor.

The Emissary was on him in seconds. Her hands jutted out and collided with his back. Zac flew forward. His head cracked against the railing along the second landing. The tubing snapped loose from the rail and clattered beside an aching Zac.

"The future will be written as designed," the Emissary said. "You simply have no place in it any longer."

Zac grabbed the pipe. He swung the metallic weapon with every last ounce of strength left to him. The pipe slammed against the Emissary's cheek. Driven back by the impact, the woman crashed to the ground.

Zac held tight to the pipe. He used it for leverage to work his way to his feet. Blood trickled from his forehead, and he dabbed at it with his free hand. The Emissary was slow to move. As she stood, Zac realized why.

Her skin had shredded from his blow. Servos and circuits whirred beneath the surface. No blood flowed from her gaping wounds, only a black fluid that sputtered out in small sprays. The Emissary wasn't human. She'd never been possessed by the protocol like the others—like the Wellspring. She was something else entirely.

"All will see the light," the Emissary said, her voice clunky as the gears of her mouth sparked from his blow. "For the First—"

A shot rang out, silencing her. The Emissary stood for a moment before she collapsed along the landing. Zac spun around to see Morgan at the base of the steps, gun in hand. Ben stood at her side, eyes locked on the Emissary.

"Morgan?" Zac called. They had made it through the drones somehow. He had sacrificed them to reach the chamber, yet they still showed up to save him.

A clicking sound woke Zac to the unfinished dilemma. Hands slapped the metal grating of the steps. The Emissary pulled herself closer to Zac, reaching for his ankle.

"She's not dying, Morgan," Ben said.

"I'm working on it," Morgan snapped.

Zac reeled away, stopped by the edge of the platform. "Work faster!"

"We promise a golden age," the Emissary said. One eye had been shattered by the bullet, the other still bright blue. "You can't stop it. We will save you all!"

Morgan and Ben shifted beneath the woman. They nodded to each other and opened fire. Bullets passed through the grating into the Emissary. Zac curled up along the edge to protect himself as best as he could from any potential ricochet.

The barrage ended in seconds. So did the Emissary's movements. She lay dead, with black ooze seeping from her wounds. Zac slowly crept closer to her body as relief filled him.

"Good luck with that."

CHAPTER THIRTY-THREE

Morgan rushed to Zac's side. Ben tried to hold back the pang of jealousy at their embrace. Even with Zac's latest betrayal, Morgan carried nothing but forgiveness for him. She had clearly learned her lesson after pushing the man away.

Ben kept his distance. He could still taste Morgan's lips on his own. Their kiss had set her free, but had done little except lock him in his own private torture session. Focusing on the dead woman sprawled along the landing helped distract him from his feelings.

Morgan called after him as he took to the stairs. "Is she—"

"Maybe." Ben crouched close to the corpse. His fingers ran along a gaping wound through her shoulder. No blood spewed from the bullet hole—only a black ooze, like oil. "She's definitely sprung a few leaks. Wouldn't want to see her mechanic's bill."

"Cute." Morgan's arm was still around Zac. Once they reached the ground floor, he pulled away.

"Zac?" Ben called. "Are you all right? What—"

Zac waved away the question. He zeroed in on a series of panels and levers along the wall. "I have to finish this. Before anything else goes wrong."

"Like us saving your ass. Again."

"Ben…" Morgan said.

Ben jumped down from the landing. His hand snared Zac's shoulder and spun the tech around. "You brought those damn drones down on us, Zac. We almost lost our lives. Morgan near-ly—"

"I had to." Zac slapped Ben's arm away. "You think I wanted that? That I wanted any of this? I need to disrupt that signal."

He pointed to the chamber above. Tears stained his cheeks.

Morgan reached out to him. "Let us help."

Her hand fell along his arm. He ran his fingers along her skin, a sad smile on his face. "You have. That's why I asked Claire to contact you, to make sure I did what had to be done. You've always been my rock — both of you. I've seen you both do such amazing things at the DSA together. I needed that strength to get me here. To help me see this through to the end."

"So, what can we do?"

"That's just it," Zac said. "You've done it. I made it this far thanks to you. Despite what you might think, I never wanted anything bad to happen to you. Ben, I called those drones so I could get here. This controls the entire spire. It's the nerve center for everything we've seen and for everything that is coming our way."

"The First," Ben said.

Zac nodded. "Whatever that might be. I wish I knew, but..." His head fell low. "I'm sorry. About before, about the choices I've made. You don't know how sorry I am."

Ben shifted closer. He saw the pain in the man's eyes, the agony Zac had carried since being abandoned by the team. They had all made mistakes and would forever be haunted by them. Zac didn't need to carry that burden alone anymore.

"I'm starting to understand," Ben said. "Apology accepted."

"Thank you," Zac whispered. He wiped his swollen eyes and stained cheeks. Moving for the controls, Zac grabbed hold of a large lever. He flipped it hard to the right. Above, energy crackled around a lone chair at the peak of the great machine in the room. "You've both given me so much. Thank you."

"You don't have to thank us, Zac," Morgan said. "We're in this together."

"I'm afraid this one is on me, Morgan."

"Why?"

"I'm the Wellspring."

Both stared at him. They'd never met the Wellspring, but had heard plenty about the enigmatic program.

"But..." Morgan stuttered. "She... She died. And then you —"

Ben pushed through Morgan's questions. He nudged Zac with his elbow. "Quite the promotion, Modine."

"Knock it off, Ben," Morgan snapped. Her brow furrowed, and her eyes scanned for some sign of what he was trying to tell them. She was ever the doctor, at work on some prognosis. "How did it happen?"

"She died, like you said," Zac said. "Someone had to carry the load."

"How do we get it out of you?" Morgan asked.

Zac pointed above to the chamber. "The field holding the signal generator in place can only be activated by certain functionaries in the system. The Emissary for maintaining the device itself, and—"

"You."

"What happens when you go in there?" Her concern grew with each unknown.

"I stop the signal," Zac replied. "It's been feeding us our future, plotting a course to an end we have no control over. I have to stop it before the signal reaches terminal point and we're too late to stop whatever the hell is coming our way. I have to, Morgan."

"We'll help," she said. "We can keep an eye on the controls, monitor your vitals. Find another way to do what you're saying."

"There is no other way." Zac shook his head. "I can do this, Morgan, but not if you're here." He stepped to the landing, away from them. "There are… security measures. Any foreign entities in the chamber when I step inside go kablooey."

"Kablooey?" Morgan said with a slight smirk.

He grinned back at her. "Big time kablooey."

Morgan embraced him once more and squeezed him tight. "God, I missed you."

Zac's hands ran along her arms, slow to fall away from her hug. "I missed you too. We can catch up as soon as I shut this down."

"You're sure you can do that?"

Zac caught Ben's stare. Sad eyes tried to find anywhere else to look, but Ben saw everything in that fleeting moment. "I have to," Zac said. "The disruption will cause a cascade effect, and wipe out towers all over the planet. No more Wellspring. Only Zac."

Morgan's smile widened at the news. Zac's, however, fell sullen. She didn't hear what he had truly said. Her own hopes and dreams obscured his words and the meaning behind them. Ben realized the truth, though. He held out his hand to the man.

"Good luck, Zac."

"Thank you," he replied, taking the hand.

"Are you sure—"

Ben let go of Zac. A gentle hold along Morgan's shoulder helped guide her toward the door. "He has a job to do. Let's leave him to it."

"Ben," Zac called.

"Yes?"

"There is an emergency stairwell on the far side of the building," he said. "The elevators are blocked. So are the main entrances. But that one is still clear. The door is marked Maintenance. Use it. Please."

"We will."

"Zac?"

"I have this, Morgan," Zac said. "I'll see you soon."

Morgan tried to resist Ben's pull for the door. She didn't want to leave Zac's side, always afraid for him—her heart fully exposed. Ben forced her into the hall; he knew their time was limited. They needed to get out of the building. Ben pushed aside any animosity toward Zac. Every jealous thought, every bit of anger and contempt toward the man, fell behind a wall of appreciation at what their friend had to do next.

It was Zac's turn to save the day.

CHAPTER THIRTY-FOUR

Zac made the slow climb back to the chamber. Every thought turned to those behind him. He quietly thanked Ben and Morgan for their timely intervention. Claire earned her own silent prayer of gratitude for her hand in bringing the DSA to his rescue. He'd been so blessed by those around him.

He wished he had appreciated them more.

Part of him worried for his loved ones, as well as his friends. All had their share of concerns for him. It wasn't an admission of doubt in his ability, just a recognition of his importance in their lives. They needed him, and always had, despite the lies Zac had used to convince himself otherwise. Whether they came from within, or had been fed to him by people like Sullivan and Hollis, Zac now recognized the truth—just as he did for what came next.

Morgan had been right to press him for answers. He had hidden the truth from her, swallowed it down for fear she would have easily convinced him to walk away from the task. That was no longer an option, and he now knew the cost of his journey.

The Wellspring had kept the secret from him. For weeks, Zac had thought disrupting the signal would end the screaming in his brain. That once the signal went dark, the Wellspring consciousness would be released, and scattered to the winds. It would be the end of the functionary role, much like the Emissary.

The Wellspring, though, had lied. The truth had come out in drips and drabs, secrets no longer able to be hidden thanks to the constant pressure Zac had maintained on the programming locked in his mind. The only person capable of entering the energy cascade was the Wellspring. To pass through the field completely meant giving in to the program.

To complete his journey, and the task set before him by April Newton, Zac had to let go of himself in the process. She had tried to make him understand, to get him to see that there was more than his own freedom at stake. His own life meant nothing compared to those he needed to save. The future was riding on Zac making the right choice for once in his life.

It's all about loyalty now.

Hearing Lincoln MacKenzie's words brought a sad smile to Zac's face. It had taken him far too long to understand the man's sentiment, and for that, there was no excuse. There was also no time like the present to rectify the many errors in judgment that plagued him of late. He knew who to believe in now, and who to trust over all others.

Zac hoped Morgan would understand in time. She would move on and realize what he noticed in her partner's eyes. It all fell to the DSA to carry on, to stop the future to come. It fell to Zac to give them a fighting chance.

His hand touched the energy cascade. He pushed his fingers through. Tingling ran up his arm and down his spine.

April stood before him in the energy. She reached out for him. "Thank you, Zac. You've helped change the world, and they don't even know it."

Zac laughed while tears streamed from his eyes. "So much for recognition, huh?" He took her hand. "Thank *you*, April, for showing me the way, and for guiding me to the right choice. My choice."

"Our choice together," she said.

Zac pushed into the energy cascade. His entire body sank through the field of blue. Sparks fluttered across his field of vision. April melted into him, both one and the same.

For a split-second, Zac saw everything. He understood the whole of the universe. The information overwhelmed his brain. The future unlocked for him, the secret of the First, and the trials ahead. He cried out for Claire and Alex. He wished he could see their faces one last time and dreamed of the day they could be together again.

Then everything went dark.

Zac Modine was gone. The Wellspring stood in his place

within the confines of the chamber. There were no more hopes and dreams, only the protocol.

Sitting upon the chair, the Wellspring lowered the helmet over his head. The signal filled his senses, but instead of embracing the download sent from his mysterious master, the Wellspring rejected the information. He pushed out with all his will, causing feedback into the system. The signal diffused outward and struggled to contain the mounting overload through the delicate mechanism at the heart of the spire.

"We serve the First and the glory to come," the Wellspring said. His voice changed; the sadness of the man broke back through to the surface as the final push sent the signal into cascade failure. Zac's words echoed in the heart of the machine. "No more."

From below, the eruptions began. The failure forced every piece of intricate machinery in the chamber to overload. It bypassed all safeties, the cascade too quick and too fierce to control or remedy. Explosions ripped through the lower levels of the room and rose incrementally. Faster and faster, the detonations consumed the Signal Chamber and the lone occupant within.

A cry echoed through the room before it fell to the flames that sparked all around and burst outward into the world with one last blast of defiance.

CHAPTER THIRTY-FIVE

Time slipped away from Hollis. He sat along the back wall of the closet and stared at the shelving that barred the door from entry. Twin automatics sat at his side, useless. The pistol clutched in his hand felt the same. He continually checked the clip to verify the full complement of bullets remained present.

This was supposed to be his day. Tracking Modine down to locate the source of the Wellspring's power was supposed to bring Hollis new insight into the future—his future. He should have been knee-deep in technology unseen by the world, or understanding fresh revelations about humanity's ultimate destiny. Instead, he cowered under the dim light of the single bulb fixture that dangled from the ceiling and waited for the drones to overtake him.

When silence fell in the hallway, Hollis' brow furrowed. He shuffled closer and quietly, working his way to his feet. He lifted a weapon from the floor. While the automatic would serve little in the long run, it might buy him some time to escape from the building.

The pounding returned, a fist against the compromised door. Hollis jumped back at the sound, then cursed at the fear he had condemned Lance for earlier. This wasn't the time to falter.

"Sir?" a voice called through the door. "Sir, are you in there?"

"Who's there?" Hollis asked, as if someone had dropped by unannounced during dinner. He cleared his throat. "Identify yourself. I have a gun trained on the door."

"It's Edelson, sir," the soldier replied.

Edelson was a sergeant among his team: a more recent recruit, but well-regarded by his superiors.

Hollis moved for the shelving. He pulled it away from the door, then stepped over the remaining debris. The door opened a crack, and Hollis stepped through.

Behind Edelson, the bodies of dozens covered the floor. Three had been his own men, including the sacrificial lamb—Lance. It had been a necessary move, yet the moment Hollis' eyes fell on the man, he forced himself to look away.

"How did you survive, soldier?"

"Several of us made it to the third floor," Edelson said. "There was minimal resistance, and we found a defensible position. We simply waited until the bastards stopped coming at us."

"Good," Hollis said. "Very good."

"Sir?" Edelson said, clearly reading Hollis' face. "Are you all right?"

The soldier passed over some water. Hollis drank a large gulp, then poured some from the bottle over his face. He rubbed it in and worked it through his hair. The cold woke him to the present. "Yes. Fine."

"We're stationed this way." Edelson led them through the swath of bodies for the stairs.

"How many?"

"Six of us."

Hollis glanced back before entering the stairwell. "And the drones stopped coming?"

Edelson shrugged. "We thought they ran out of manpower at first."

"But that wasn't the case?"

"No," the soldier said. "When we inspected the second floor, there were bodies in offices that hadn't even been activated. It's like they shut down."

Hollis nodded. Whatever, or whoever, had instituted the failsafe must have been taken out of the equation. Without direction, the patchwork army fell where they stood.

Edelson held the door to the third floor and ushered Hollis inside. He scanned the corridor cautiously. "Why here?"

"I'm sorry, sir?"

"Why remain on this floor?" Edelson rubbed his neck at the question, clearly unsure where to begin. Hollis pushed ahead, a knowing gleam in his eye. "You've found something, haven't you?"

"Yes, sir."

A devilish grin spread across Hollis' face. All sense of defeat, of powerlessness at the hands of the future tech in the mysterious spire, vanished. His true purpose returned in a flash, and so did his confidence.

"Show me."

Edelson escorted Hollis down the hall. They stopped at a lone door in the center and entered. The room within was a lab suite that extended the entire length of the building. Stations were set up throughout, and a conveyor belt for processing looped above them to a packaging area in the corner.

Computer terminals lit up before the soldiers already gathered. They worked to remove hard drives and secure data. Edelson led Hollis deeper into the room. He pointed ahead.

"As near as we can tell, this was their main research area," Edelson said. "Supplies and equipment were delivered via a tunnel to the neighboring structure."

Hollis saw the conveyance on the far side of the building. There had been no sign of it from their approach to the front; the illusion of the condemned building had obscured the true nature of the property.

"We've requested more hands from local assets," Edelson continued. To the soldier, it was an attempt to show initiative. To Hollis, however, reaching outside the room meant opening the door to trouble.

"There's no time," Hollis said. "Call them off so as not to alert any interference."

"Sir?"

"The fail-safe that triggered within those drones has been taken out. There is no telling what might come next. Or what happens to all of this if we don't move swiftly to secure as much as possible."

Hollis followed the trail of the conveyor belt to the packaging center. His hand dug through the boxes of goods ready for transit.

Another soldier stepped forward. "Be careful, sir."

Falling from the box was a dermal patch, just like those worn by the drones throughout the building. Hollis grabbed a glove from a nearby station and slipped it on before he retrieved the dropped patch.

"Incredible," he whispered. "To think such technology has been within reach this entire time."

"Sir!" a soldier exclaimed from the center of the room. "I found a terminal unlocked. Full access available."

"Download every schematic, every blueprint, and file," Hollis said. He put the patch within the open box, then patted the lid shut. "Take what you can carry."

A tremor rocked the structure. The entire building shook from the force, rattling the soldiers, who struggled to remain upright. Reverberations calmed seconds later, yet Hollis continued to glance upward, wary of what might have occurred.

"Move quickly, gentlemen," Hollis ordered. He started for the tunnel at the far end of the room. This was what he expected to find, the destiny he had sought for so long. A smile ran across his face. "Today, we ensure humanity's future."

CHAPTER THIRTY-SIX

A kick sent the emergency exit flying open. Ben pulled Morgan along, clearly determined to keep her with him at all times during their flight from the building. Morgan went along with it, too scattered to think straight.

Zac was still inside. She had found him, had rescued him from danger, yet abandoned him again. She wanted to scream. The entire trip down to ground level, all she wanted was to let go of her partner, and race back to the central chamber—threat be damned.

Back outside in the fresh air, Ben continued to race away from the building. Morgan's disjointed thoughts turned to concern at the distance being put between them and the spire. Ben didn't stop until they were across the street. His chest heaved, and he fought to catch his breath from the hasty retreat.

Morgan shifted away from him. She staggered to the edge of the sidewalk and stared up at the incredible spire. Zac had asked her to leave, to finish the task set before him. None of it sat right with Morgan, and the last thing she could handle was another mistake added to the many made today.

"I'm going back," she announced.

Ben shook his head. He jumped in front of her to block her path. "No, you're not."

Her fists clenched tight at her sides. "We never should have left him."

"He asked us to, Morgan," Ben replied. "It was the right call."

"Something was wrong," she said. "I could feel it. He wasn't telling us everything."

"Yes, he was," Ben said. "You just didn't want to hear it."

"What do you mean?" Her brow furrowed. "Tell me, Ben. What the hell do you mean?"

"Please," her partner said. "There wasn't another way."

Morgan's eyes widened. She pushed through Ben. "To hell with it. I'm going back for Zac. I need to—"

The explosion ripped through the midsection of the building. Glass and metal blew out from the blast. Flames erupted from the structure's exposed innards. The building groaned and metallic beams threatened to collapse under the pressure of the blast. The sky above filled with pieces of the spire, like metallic raindrops falling to the earth.

Ben grabbed Morgan by the shoulder, then yanked her away from the street. "Look out!"

Debris slammed into the ground. The road cracked from the impact, and the pieces scattered in all directions. Ben shielded Morgan from the small chunks that bounded for their position.

Morgan's eyes, though, never left the spire. Four floors burned; the flames rose into the sky. "That's... that's where we were," she stammered. "That's where—"

Ben turned away.

"Zac!" she bellowed. Tears streamed down her cheeks. "ZAC!"

Morgan's fists pounded against his chest. Ben took the beating in stride. He never faltered and refused to let her go for an instant. "He did what he had to, Morgan. Zac took out the signal. He did it."

"Let me go." She decked him against the cheek. Ben fell to the ground. "He might still be alive. I can—"

"He's gone, Morgan," Ben said, swiping at the wound. He reached for her hand. Morgan, however, kept her distance. "We have to go, too. The Trust is all over the building. This isn't over."

"It is for some of us."

Tears filled her eyes. Memories flooded her senses. Every one contained an image of Zac, and every one threatened to cripple her where she stood. She never had a chance with the man— their one night together the only moment of peace against the raging storm the world sent crashing against them to split them apart.

They had been fated to fail, just like her so-called leadership of the DSA. Two men had died under her watch. Her first mission as leader, and the bodies spoke to her effectiveness at the task.

Morgan screamed. Every ounce of rage and despair blew out of her with as much force as the explosion that took Zac from her. She wanted to crumble, to surrender. As her knees gave way, though, a hand pulled her back to her feet.

Ben stood at her side. He was always at her side. "Morgan, please. They're coming. We have to—"

Screeching tires skidded to a halt next to them. The headlights were cracked, and the paint job ruined, but they immediately recognized the van. Kanigher opened the passenger side door and waved them over.

"Get in."

Ben moved for the van. He stopped when he realized he was alone. "Morgan?"

She was lost in the fire burning above. They learned nothing about the building, or about what the signal truly meant. Nothing made sense to her, only what she had lost because of her ignorance.

Morgan bowed her head, a silent prayer to Zac on her lips. Slowly, she joined Ben in the van.

"Get us out of here."

Kanigher nodded. The van shifted into gear, and they headed away from the blaze. Morgan looked into the mirror one last time at the final resting place of Zac Modine, and whispered, "Goodbye."

CHAPTER THIRTY-SEVEN

Most were quiet in the van. The day's events had shaken everyone. Kanigher had relayed the siege at their safe house, just as Ben and Morgan shared their experiences with Davey and Zac.

When Ben finished telling the sullen driver about Zac's sacrifice, Adler stirred from her seat. She had been curled in the back, knees tucked tight to her chest. In a flurry of motion, she grabbed her belongings to retrieve her tablet. Adler tapped feverishly at the screen. Ben shifted closer, curious as to her actions.

"It's gone," she whispered, a hand to her lips.

"Adler?"

"All that searching, all that wondering, and now it's just gone…" Adler lowered the tablet, then dropped it atop her bag. "The signal isn't being picked up on any scans."

"Good."

"We never learned anything about it," Adler said. "Never figured out what it meant to accomplish."

"The Wellspring was using it," Ben replied. "Zac told us as much. If the signal was being used by the Wellspring, that means it was a tool of the Trust. I say, it being gone is a very good thing."

"I don't know. I wish I did, but… I just don't know," Adler muttered. She stared off into the distance. Ben moved to console her. At his approach, Adler shrank farther into the seat. Her body shook with fear, like she had been ready to jump out of the van at the thought of being touched. Whatever had happened to her in the safe house refused to subside. Ben wondered if it ever would.

Ben looked around at the others. From Holbrook's silence to Morgan's tears, and back again, he noted all of their shared pain. "I get it," he said. "This was not our day. Not with what we've suffered. What we've lost. But despite the pain, despite those not here with us right now, we won. The signal is gone, and can't be used—either by the Trust or whoever this First thing is. We won."

No one turned to him. No slow clap of acceptance brought them all together. There was only sorrow, encapsulated perfectly by Morgan as she crumpled against her seat.

"It sure as hell doesn't feel that way."

"Yeah, well, if you don't feel that way now, it's about to get worse," Kanigher said.

A blockade wrapped around the next intersection. Local police, in conjunction with military units, cordoned off the entire area.

Kanigher slammed on the brakes. Ben leaned forward. "Back it up, Kanigher. Back it up now!"

The driver's eyes thinned at the sight caught in the side mirror. "Shit."

"What?"

Morgan shook her head. "Backing up is not an option."

Sirens blared behind them. Six patrol cars raced toward their position. They caught up fast while the van sat still in the middle of the road.

"This isn't good," Ben said.

A bullhorn at the cordon squawked, and a voice roared down the street. "Vacate your vehicle with your hands over your heads. Fail to do so, and we will be forced to open fire."

Adler closed her eyes tightly. She rocked slowly in her chair. "What do we do?"

"It's the Trust," Kanigher said. "The military detachment is from General Adams' camp."

"And they've pulled in local law enforcement," Morgan said.

Ben grumbled. "God forbid they don't pin the huge, exploding building on us."

Kanigher tightened along the wheel. He glanced in the rearview mirror. "What's the play, Morgan?" Silent surprise passed between them. This was not the time for a power struggle in the group. "I can gun it. Clear out a path. Van might not last long after, though. If it does at all."

"That would give us a chance to find a place to lie low. Buy us time to think," Ben said with a nod of agreement. "Morgan?"

He knew the answer the moment he saw her eyes. They were still locked on Zac—lost on the dead. She shook her head. "We surrender."

"You can't—" Ben started, then caught himself.

Morgan shot him a glare. "No one else is dying on my watch, Ben." She moved for the side panel door. Opening it, she led with her hands open and up in the air. "We're coming out!"

Kanigher beat his fist against the steering wheel. Her decision obviously didn't sit well with him. Ben felt the same way. However, both lifted their hands and stepped out of the vehicle. Adler and Holbrook joined them.

"Smart choice," a soldier called. A detachment broke from the cordon to surround the field team. Their weapons stayed trained on Ben and the others every step of the way. The lead soldier, the name Linton emblazoned on his uniform, had a thick head of hair that ran down his back. An even thicker mustache curled over his lips.

"Smarter than that mullet, at any rate," Ben replied. "How does anyone take you seriously with that thing? Respect for the stache, though. I've tried to grow mine out, but damn, does it itch after a week or two."

Linton grinned. "You must be Ben Riley. My boss would like a word."

"Send him out," Ben said. "I love a good chat."

A shadow slipped from the cordon. "You always did have trouble with that mouth, Ben."

Ben's eyes widened. "No. It can't be."

Streetlights on both sides brought her into focus. She wore a flak jacket and carried a pistol at her side. There was no need to take aim, no need to worry about anything from Ben.

After all, Ben had been looking for her for months. He had searched through databases, rummaged through empty homes, and worried himself to death over her disappearance. He could never have imagined that she would be standing in front of him as his enemy. Yet, she had been with the Trust the whole time.

Emily Wright grinned at a dumbfounded Ben Riley. "I hear you've been looking for me."

ACKNOWLEDGEMENTS

As always, this book would not be possible without the support of my incredible patrons:

Matt Patrick
Sally Hall
Sara Frandina
Paul Sardella

A special thank you goes out to my lovely wife, Melinda, and my dear friend, Vicki, for their feedback on the evolution of the Ben-Morgan relationship.

There were plenty of arguments back and forth. Their passion for the characters and this world helped strengthen the season as a whole, and I am forever in their debt for that.

ABOUT THE AUTHOR

Lou Paduano is the author of the Greystone series of urban fantasy adventures, which follow Detective Greg Loren and Soriya Greystone as they hunt myths, monsters, and legends in the city of Portents.

He is also the author of the conspiracy thriller series, The DSA, a serialized tale about a clandestine government agency trying to discover the true power behind humanity's future.

Lou lives with his wife and three daughters in Grand Island, NY. You can learn more about his books, including upcoming releases and free content by visiting his website at loupaduano.com.

THE GREYSTONE SAGA

AVAILABLE NOW

Follow the adventures of Soriya Greystone and
Detective Greg Loren as they hunt dangerous
myths and legends in the city of Portents.

BOOK ONE - SIGNS OF PORTENTS
BOOK TWO - TALES FROM PORTENTS
BOOK THREE - THE MEDUSA COIN
BOOK FOUR - PATHWAYS IN THE DARK
BOOK FIVE - A CIRCLE OF SHADOWS

GREYSTONE-IN-TRAINING

AVAILABLE NOW

For years, Soriya trained to become the Greystone.
Follow the trials that made her the protector
Portents needed to fend off the darkest of threats.

BOOK ONE - HAMMER AND ANVIL
BOOK TWO - THE GIFTS OF KALI
BOOK THREE - THE FINAL GAUNTLET